FAIRY and ODDITIES

EZRA WILLIAMS

To Kenneth,
With love and respect,
x
x Ezra Williams x
x

TSL Publications

The sight of all those expensive cars rolling along, crammed to the bulwarks with overfed males and females with fur coats and double chins, made him feel, he tells me, that he wanted to buy a red tie and a couple of bombs and start the Social Revolution. If Stalin had come along at that moment, Mervyn would have shaken him by the hand.

Well, there is, of course, only one thing for a young man to do when he feels like that. Mervyn hurried along to the club and in rapid succession drank three Martini cocktails.

The treatment was effective, as it always is …

P. G. Wodehouse - *Mulliner Nights*

… I was looking for a job, not a love affair. I did not find work. Instead I found the *grande amore*, the kind of love that changes your life overnight, where things go from black and white to vibrant color.

Erica Heller - *Yossarian Slept Here*

For Eli, as always,
and to Sylva Klojdová for being there, and there still.
And in loving memory of my dear friends
David Hyde and Gary Hughes.

Contents

The King of the Cats

Cyril Williams was a gravedigger. He had fought during World War II in Burma and had been court-martialed and imprisoned for driving a tank through the Officers' Mess Hall. His mental ailments had continued in civilian life, but he was not, at heart, a bad man. He beat his wife, Kathleen, for money to buy beer, it's true, but always in his heart he secretly thought he would change. He hoped to, and perhaps sometimes this is all we have. And hope is a good thing, possibly the best thing.

One cold evening — the kind that numbs your bones and makes you consider what your freezing point would be — Kathleen was waiting for Cyril to come home. She was by the fireside and their cat, Tom, who was white with a black spot on his chest, nestled in her lap. Tom was almost asleep, richly breathing with half-purrs on the exhalations; Kathleen's head nodded as she remembered the times before the war. Not quite the happy times, but certainly the happier times, for them.

She had waited for many hours but still Cyril didn't come home. He wasn't at the pub. She knew this. He was working, digging the grave of Father Smythe, the local priest who had 'passed away' the previous weekend. He had been found in a room above the local pub. A woman of 'ill-repute' had raised the alarm. No one had enquired how she came to know.

Finally Kathleen fell asleep, her chin resting on the buttoned neck of her now-grey nine-year-old blouse. Sleeves smocked at the wrists. Thinking of times before the war always sent her slowly to sleep. She would make up scenarios, or embellish pleasant real ones. This evening she had been thinking of when they had been trying for children. They had been happy then, briefly. Then war had broken out and he had come home with a kitten in one pocket and a loaf of bread in the other. Snow was curling in his hair. 'Bread is the staff of life,' he said, and placed the kitten on the floorboards where it flounced, unafraid. Kicking up dustballs. She'd loved him then.

Suddenly Cyril came in, dropping his spades across the threshold. This was something he never did — he considered it bad luck to bring any of the 'dirt of the dead' into the house.

'Who's Tom Tildrum?' he shouted. The cat leapt out and cringed into a corner. Kathleen gathered herself, patting down a momentary flare of bad temper, and replied:

'What on earth is the matter? Are you feeling all right?' She knew better than to ask him if he'd been drinking.

'Who's Tom Tildrum?' Cyril repeated.

'I have no idea,' said Kathleen. 'Who is he?'

Cyril threw down his cap and pulled out a chair from the kitchen table. The kitchen was really part of the same room, but they marked it off by using the table as the border between them. They ate in a neutral zone.

'I've had the most awful night. I can hardly believe it myself.' He poured himself a little whisky into a large dirty glass that was chipped on one side, as if someone with wide-spaced strong teeth had bitten it. Inverted, the glass resembled the pumpkins they saw families put outside their houses at Hallowe'en. They had never had cause to carve a pumpkin. In fact, neither of them had ever even held a pumpkin.

'What happened? You startled me,' said Kathleen.

'I was working on Father Smythe's grave ...' He sipped. 'Then — I hadn't dropped off, but I was ... frightened by a sound. *I know*, I know. It was like a miaow, a cat's miaow.'

Kathleen looked sadly deflated. Her life was this, tonight. Tom, their cat, emerged from the corner to sit beside a brown chair with stuffing erupting from its underside. He looked content there, with tendrils of material dangling beside him.

'So, dear?'

'Well,' replied Cyril, 'I looked across, toward the rail tracks, where the sound had come from, and I couldn't believe it. The moon was behind. Do you know what I saw?'

'I have no idea, dear.' She smiled at the rhyme. Small things pleased her. Cyril noticed that her hair had started to grey a little at the crown. He still loved her, and was sorry for all the things he'd done and could never apologise for. He continued:

'You won't believe me, but I'll tell you anyway. Nine black cats, the bloody opposite of Tom — I swear, they all had white spots on their chests — were coming towards me. But that's not the weird part.' The gravedigger put down his glass and wiped his wide bald forehead on a tattered twelve-year-old sleeve.

'What was the weird part?' asked his wife. 'That you counted them?' She didn't ask this so much as gently put it between them. She wouldn't judge.

He shook his shiny head. 'They were carrying a small coffin. No, I swear, don't get up. They were: a small coffin. I know coffins. You know I know coffins. This one was covered with a velvet pall — I saw it glistening black in the moonlight, I swear. And on the pall was a gold coronet. It looked gold — I don't know if it was real, but I couldn't move. They were *marching*, Kathy, in step. Hell, damn, they miaowed together.'

Kathleen didn't move fast. This was a difficult atmosphere. She felt he could break at any moment, flail or upend the table. She rose and smoothed his shoulders. She didn't knead: he was boyishly ticklish and didn't enjoy her seeing him in that vulnerable state. Having spent many nights alone with only Tom for company, Kathleen fantasised that when cats knead your body, they are not really kneading: they are checking your internal organs for damage. It was sweet, romantic even. She knew to smooth, not knead.

Tom jumped on to her empty seat by the fire and curled into a capital C.

Kathleen demurred, then moved round the table into the kitchen and ran herself a glass of tepid water from the rusty tap. Their sink had only one that worked. Cyril poured another inch of whisky. She said to him:

'Are you nearly ready for bed, dear?'

'Listen woman, damn, I'm not finished. They came closer and closer and I could make them out more distinctly. It's bright anyway, tonight. But their eyes had a light, a sort of spooky green light, and they all came towards me, carrying this coffin, and the biggest one of all led the group from the front.'

Kathleen sighed inwardly — Cyril wouldn't see. She wondered if this was how things were going to be from now on. At least he wasn't angry, she supposed, yet. And it was five minutes to midnight. If midnight passed, Cyril rarely flared. His body had its own routine since the war. Perhaps this was why men had invented clocks. She felt sure it was men: a woman wouldn't need a timepiece. We are timekeepers, she thought, we keep time in our bodies. Or at least I used to.

'So what happened?' she said, softly.

Cyril looked at her with an honest, haunted look she was unfamiliar with. Could he have been drinking some new drink, a spirit he'd never drunk before? It was out of character, but one could never be totally sure with a drinker. He said:

'They just advanced towards me, kept coming and coming, I swear ...' He trailed off and threw back the penultimate inch of whisky. 'Then, when they were right opposite Father Smythe's open grave — I hadn't finished it, see — they all stood still and stared at me. I was more frightened than I've ever been in my life. Ever. Do you see what I'm saying, Kathy?'

She understood. This was different. Her husband had experienced something that had reminded him of the war and it was her job, her duty, to take care of him now. She opened her arms and pulled him to her. She was still standing, so he pressed his head to her chest, in between her warm, never-suckled breasts. From above, she thought, his head looked like a clearing in a forest: fringed on three sides by trees, red and blue rows of flowers bloomed. She kissed him in the middle of the clearing and, as she did so, Tom stretched on the chair. Chest puffed-out and claws extended.

'They all stood there, looking at me with that green gaze. It was ... I don't know. The big one who wasn't carrying the coffin — they were four on each side, did I tell you? — the big one came forward and looked right in my face. But this is the worst bit ...'

Kathleen put her palms flat on either side of his face, cupping his cheeks the way she knew he liked, and bent her body down to him. She smelled his warm damp skull. They had been through so much life together, or that which passes for life, the scraps it tosses you to gnaw on till you scream for more, or less, of the same. Either way, it's certainly all you're going to get. She bent over him and felt love flood her stomach.

'The big one came forward and ... spoke.' He felt her flinch, but held tighter. Neither of them saw the cat sit up. 'It said, and its voice was squeaky but at the same time it rumbled like a mountainslide: "Tell Tom Tildrum, Tim Toldrum's dead". I *swear* that's what the bloody thing said. Tell Tom Tildrum Tim Toldrum's dead. But who is Tom Tildrum? And how can I go back out there? They're still waiting — look!'

And then he drew her to the little curtain-less window. Silhouetted against the railway tracks Kathleen saw the shapes of eight cats standing over a small coffin, and closer, a much larger one, staring impatiently back at them.

She looked her husband in the eyes and kissed him with vigour. He kissed her back, as he used to, before the war had put something impassable there, some slab, gunmetal-grey. Her smocked sleeves found their way round his neck, behind his mottled head.

On the chair Tom began to tremble — his limbs shot out, straight as splints. He drew himself up, regarded the embracing human couple by the window, acknowledged the light of the moon, and miaowed. The couple turned.

'If Tim Toldrum's dead, then I, Tom Tildrum, am now the King of the Cats. If you don't mind, I won't go up the chimney. After all, you don't have one. With respect, would you be so kind as to open the door for me?'

Cyril and Kathleen, still embracing, flipped the latch. Tom Tildrum, with a triumphant *frish* of his tail, stepped outside. The last inch of whisky sat undrunk on the table. Cyril didn't notice it. He was too busy kissing his bride.

They were young again.

The Town That Will Never Be Completed

Prologue

People tell me I often look like an old frog. Frogs, to my mind, possess a subtle humour. Not conventionally pretty perhaps, but wily. We know how to survive. Other times, people tell me I look like a grumpy walrus. Although some would argue walruses always look grumpy (or at least highly strung), I would counter that they are also lazy rolling creatures, inclined to thinking too little, butting heads and snoring. So, as I said, sometimes I look like a frog and sometimes like a walrus.

* * * *

I have lived in Owl Mist Lake for well over a thousand years. People scoff at this, tell me it's impossible, too long, a lie, and that I'm a 'funny old dog'. There — animals again — why does this happen to me? How do they know whether a thousand years is a long or a short time? Can *you* tell? Of course you can't. So you have no reason to disbelieve me. If I told you that I had lived so long because of some superior wisdom then you could correctly call me a fraud. But it seems that I've always been here by my beautiful lake. And like most beautiful things, my lake has a sorrowful history.

Many boots have trampled this place: mostly armies, from here and there. These guys in red, those guys in white or blue — but also fleeing refugees, the exiled, visiting dignitaries, aristocrats, sects, chanters, dancers, money-spinners, tall-tale tellers, dot com entrepreneurs, drunkards, fools, and those who believe in gods. Chipped communist stones litter my lake's stale banks.

Even the name Owl Mist has a sorrowful pang, at least for me. It may be that I'm the last one to ever care. It's a mistranslation from the Elobian. It *should* be Oil Mist, as in the smoke that hangs then drifts after some oil has been aflame, or is still aflame, somewhere, hopefully controlled. But some stupid man — they are always men — mixed up oil and owl, so I now live in a misnamed lake. But enough of such sadnesses.

I'm getting old of course, so I'll keep things brisk. I won't tell a long and very serious story. Just what happened, or occurred as they increasingly say these days, in chunks small enough to swallow. I hope you enjoy my story, and the little part I play in it. I'm not one to boast. And of course, if you're ever passing my way, look me up. Sorry, a correction. I meant to say — look up! I'll probably still be here by Owl Mist Lake. I bet you'd like it here. The growing walls talk. And, if I'm not around, you can look for me in them, or in the water, cold and stylish, or in the sound the leaves make as they brush the water.

* * * *

The text (translated into English from the Elobian) that appears by an exhibit in the town's eponymous History Museum:

The Town That Will Never Be Completed

Every spring at some dark night an old little grey man emerges from Lake Owl Mist, goes downhill and reaching the gates of the town, asks the watchman: 'Has the town been completed already?'

All the watchmen, however, have been compelled by the court of law to give the answer: 'No, the town is far from ready. There is much to be built yet and it will take a good many years before everything is finished.'

The old man would shake his grizzled head and mutter in frustration, turn around and return to his lake. Should the watchman accidentally reply that the town is quite ready, the old man would send the waters of Owl Mist down into the valley where

the town is situated and drown
everything and everybody in it.

* * * *

My story concerns a girl named Lina and the events that happened
— occurred be damned! — at the Town Song Contest last spring.
At least I think it was last spring. I am old, you know. It must have
been: I remember all the flaxen nubile totty, daughters of the
guildsmen mostly, lined up by the stage. Singing itself was a
national tradition. It had even overcome the last occupation. They
called it the Singing Revolution — the power of many voices
joined in a quest for freedom. Those songs were still sung, albeit
by a generation with little understanding of the ideology. To these
the old listened sadly, or with tiredness, but without complaining.
The voice was the very first musical instrument after all. You sang
to attract a mate. But the past is a musical line too ... Let's not beat
about here, hje hje.

Before we proceed on, a quick word about my potty mouth.
There is a strain of old men (to which I firmly belong) who, when
confronted by collegiate and quite lovely pink female flesh, let their
mouths run away with them. So, if you find me putting my foot in
it from time to time, don't be too harsh. I'm unused to the company.

So. Unless death had come calling or a new baby been born that
day, everybody turned out for the Song Contest. It was an occasion
not only for the town to get together in their finest, and boast and
drink, but to determine the strategic marriage matches of many
young fragrant townspeople, announce auspicious new engag-
ments, swap felicitous church gossip, barter for trade deals, and
much else besides. There were clowns, jugglers, hawkers, great
magicians. Holy men smeared with ash. Warm wine with berries
was served in crinkly plastic cups. Tourists milled about, with
exceptional cameras. Click everything. Huge-arsed foreign girls
clung to arms in leather jackets with warm, slightly desperate
expressions. The next time they slept with their boyfriends, they'd
pretend to not enjoy it. Warm gulps in oft-breathed air.

I hadn't been down to the town since last year you see, or so I think — time is curved. I was feeling swiltchy, bulby, out of sorts, not yet ready to mingle with the crowds. Yet hearing Lina's sweet voice carried on the musky air made me long to see succulent smooth thighs tapering heavenward, big fluffy boots below. My old, old heart beat faster, hje hje, to think on such things.

So I got myself together, polished my tusks and all that dross, and emerged from Owl Mist Lake. My beard was garlanded with weeds, dripping shyly. I made my way downhill, with careful tread, as my bones were creaking. Plop plop said my beard, crawk yaw replied my bones. A few hours (or days — who really understands these things?) brought the gates of the town into view. They were heavy wood, darkly knotted and fifteen inches thick, with a moist sheen to them. The sign above them read Virtu Gate.

The watchman I hadn't met before. He was a stout, almost square man, and his name badge read Walther. But, wouldn't you know, what with my voice being silent for so long, so rusty, so unused, the sound that issued forth from my throat was more like *wanker* than *Walther*.

He started, as well he might, and drew his sword, but re-sheathed it after croaky apologies on my part.

I really was a spectacle. Doddery, stuttering, raspy. Useless husk. So, it was with a colossal effort of will and drawing myself to full height, that I demanded to know whether the town had been completed already.

'Has the town been completed already?' I thundered. In reality, it was more of a nervous mewl, but one needs to get psyched up for such nonsense.

The watchman sniggered and, waving his right forefinger, said: 'Yo, dude, you fucking mental or wot?'

'No indeedy,' quoth I, 'I merely want to know if the town has been completed already.' I did that interrogative rise at the end that young humans seem to respond to.

Lina's full voice could be heard coming through the gates and it lightened the atmosphere for us both. Totes fly and chill. It was a rare instrument — subtle yet taut, rich and dancing. And so sensual — curving phrases like budding breasts. Hje hje, there I go again.

Walther looked at me solidly. 'What's all this claptrap? You

pulling my daisy?' Pointing over his shoulder to the slender sentry box just inside the town doors, he continued: 'I got a halberd in there dude, and I'm itching, like *really* itching to use it ...'

'Dear boy, I say unto you: Has the town been completed already? Oh, for fuck's sake. Is the work finished? Have the builders gone to blow their wads on booze? Clear? Hje. Hje.'

'Fuck man, why didn't you say so? Sorry. No idea.' He didn't pronounce it idea, he pronounced it id-eea, like the beginning of idiot followed by a leer. 'Clue-frigging-less. What you care anyway?'

'Don't you know who I am?' Yes, yes, I felt bad asking this. I've always despised the antics of mediocre celebrities and didn't enjoy the *frisson* of feeling like one. Still ... 'Didn't your parents tell you of the Old Frog?'

Walther looked dubious. Or doubtful. Hard to tell. Lantern-jawed and dull-eyed, he seemed the kind of man who would view a pretty chaffinch on a tree branch and a vicious rape with the same detachment. In fact, he'd most likely have been committing the vicious rape.

'Didn't they frighten you at bedtime with tales of the Old Frog? No? Well, that's me, that is. I'm the Old Frog.'

'Piss off.' He was flabbergasted.

'No, seriously — I *am* the Old Frog, ask anyone. Actually, no, don't. Look, all I need is a *yea* or a *nay* to my question. Just answer quickly. Come on.'

'I better check with Human Resources ...'

'Walther, old chum, come come. Think of me as an uncle you don't see that often. The one who brings the best presents on those Christmases he does make. After all, you have known me, in a way, your whole life, now haven't you?'

'Yo, but they say you is a monster, like.'

'That's very good, Walther,' I replied in an indulgent, avuncular tone, 'but you know better, don't you? You've actually met me, and I'm not a monster now, am I? A bit fuzzy around the edges perhaps, a bit gnarled of hand and crooked of tooth, deep-browed, wiry hair on my chinny chin chin ...' I was waxing lyrical. This rarely helped a situation. 'But scary? A monster? Surely — *no.*'

Walther seemed to be blinking in Morse code. He scratched his chinny chin chin with the ear-end of the landline receiver he had withdrawn from the guardhouse entrance. I continued rapidly: 'Now I'll be on my way just as quick as you can say "want not, want not", if you'd be kind and answer my question.'

The lunk looked wary. Some law, a law that all the watchmen must abide by, was stretching itself and yawning across his blancmange brain. His instincts were spot on — possibly why he'd got the job in the first place — but Walther was a woefully slow fellow, unless gyms or violence were involved. Crossword puzzles were enemies.

I looked at my wrist (where a watch could have been) and tapped my foot, smiling without cease. TV-brightness. Square yellow teeth. Eventually he said:

'No, the town is far from ready. There is much to be built yet and it will take a good many years before everything is finished.'

He looked as astounded as I probably did. What devilry, what freakishness was this? My blood was rising like farts in water. Bubble bubble, soil and stubble. But I was thinking clearly, more clearly indeed than at any previous time, and I had hatched a plan.

I smote him with a quick flash of my tusks, gutted him right there on the cobbled path that looked like rain. His innards continued to pulse on the ground as I strode over them and on into the town.

Thank goodness everyone was at the Song Contest and didn't see Walther's demise or, more importantly, hear what he'd said.

By now several male voices were singing in harmony, two tenor lines and two bass. Their voices were like walking into a deep dark forest. As I approached the Town Hall Square, I hid in the shadows for a moment to observe the scene.

A smallish stage, fifteen-feet by ten, had been erected to the left of the Town Hall, which filled the whole right side of the square from where I stood. The modest proscenium arch was decorated with little white and blue flags and twinkly plastic branches. The judges' chairs were positioned in front of the stage in a crescent, the crowd jostling behind them.

The judges were the most important men in town, all guildsmen of course, and they were dressed in richly red, folded garments with gold frills around the sleeves. Each outfit bore some symbol of the wearer's profession. There were butchers with embroidered trotters, tailors with fancy epaulettes, thatchers with threaded twigs. Coppersmiths, members of the clergy, journeymen, potters. Each had a small table with a slate and chalk for noting down marks on the performances, and a tankard of beer. I noticed the tankards were also embossed with signs of their users' professions. The clergyman's had an angel for a handle. I hoped there were devil horns, sweating somewhere nearby.

Head Judge, and Alderman of the Guild, was Lina's father, Hans Kansa, who (with the exception of the actual Prime Minister of Elobia) was arguably the most important man in the town. No deals were done without his say-so, no new business thrived without his nod. He was the master builder, and the man who was, at least to my eyes, responsible for the town's burgeoning growth. Each year my hatred of him grew.

Even up by my lake, over the last year, several apartment blocks had sprung up with huge coloured shatterproof-glass rectangles on the sides. The eastern bank of Owl Mist had been golf course-sloped, the landscape 'contoured' for aesthetic effect. Twelve ducks' nests and three swans' nests were destroyed for this. I knew their remotest antecedents. Opposite the apartment blocks, and slowly leaking pollutants into my water, was a graveyard for discarded lorries. Disused pipes, pilfered engines and chimneys lazed about, the odd sparrow carcass in a wheel-hub.

Owl Mist was a similar shape to the town that lay in the valley below. Broadly oval and wider at the western end (corresponding to the town's fortifications), it ran to a bottleneck at the opposite end, where there were layered rocky formations. The ravens there were not purely black like they are where you live — they had grey breasts and backs. They looked sprightly on my rocks. Then a long metal barrier with wildlife-viewing signs appeared — the cheek! — facing the apartment blocks over yonder. A discrete nameless island is featured some metres from the bottleneck on some maps. Some millions of years ago (who can ever say with certainty?) this channel led to a much larger lake. But not even I go back that far.

Just before stepping into the bustle of the square to begin my plan, I turned at the sound of several sharp flaps. Two pigeons were duelling in a doorway, pecking and tearing at each other. Eventually one managed to wedge its head underneath the wing of the other and began to twist, presumably to break it. The fighter with the broken wing would starve if it couldn't fly, crawl off to some dark corner. I began to smile, with glittering cruelty. I didn't have time to witness the outcome of that avian rumble, but I did notice a female bird perched some feet away, following the action carefully. Yeah, I thought, the things we do for you, little power.

* * * *

The singers had finished and Hans Kansa stepped up on to the platform to announce the judges' retirement for discussion when I came out. Hje hje. I stepped forward into the light, voice raised, affectedly hoarse yet overpowering in virility and lurching cadences. This from a very old man, too. I'm not sure how old, to be exact, but certainly old. Think on that if you will. The crowd turned, the young startled, the old (saddened by the youngs' songs) staring in terror as if jackboots had come again, instead of just their Old Frog.

'What ho,' I thundered — no, I really did thunder this time — I was in fine fettle, totally psyched, all now roused and prowly-like. 'What do I see here? Is the contest over? Do I not merit entertainment?'

Hans Kansa patted the air to quieten the tittering maidens (hje hje) on either side of the flimsy stage in their pink, green, yellow, cream and peach dresses. What was underneath that cloth ... Silken honey-fragrant skin, panties the consistency of frowns. Sorry, I should stop thinking such thoughts. The guildsmen scraped their chairs round on the cobbles to observe me. The Song Contest Prize Cup, handle the shape of a smitheringale standing on a deer's foot was stage centre forward, in front of old Kansa.

He was a many-panelled man. The correct tone was set. Personal charm was forced, tele-visual, falsely bright in his face. This is what we want. From previous visits I knew him to be universally

25

cordial, but, upon hearing my voice, I had never seen so discouraged a fellow.

'Continue on, old chum,' I continued, playing with my beard menacingly, a finger there, a finger here, to discourage interruption. 'I very much enjoy the view of your new blocks on the banks of my lake. Your colourful squares, or are they oblongs? No matter. *My lake*, I hear you say. Oh yes, *hooooeeeee*. In case you didn't recognise me, I am your Old Frog, the Walrus himself, the old man of Owl Mist. I have come here tonight to tell you that just this minute, or some minutes ago, I mean who knows really, right? Some time back, the watchman at Virtu Gate informed me that the town was indeed finished. He said: "The town is quite ready". He is now dead. I smote him and watched his delicious bubbling ...' I caught myself before the tendency to wax lyrical took over. It never helped. Did I tell you that?

Why had I never thought of this before? It was so simple to pretend. There were caterwauling protests from the crowd, and some sobbing on the maidens' front — I got the feeling Walther was a prized specimen — but Hans Kansa silenced them with a swipe of his rich arms.

For a few centuries (I think — do you know for sure?) the town had had a habit of leaving stubby candles burning in circular pots on their doorsteps, to signal that a shop or an eatery was open for custom. I noticed many of these had been hastily blown out. Thin greasy smoke rose from the sides of the crowd. I barely paused:

'So, here I am. The town is quite ready and so am I. But I have a proposition for you, a wager if you prefer — *I* do. I like a good wager — which may be able to stop me sending the waters of Owl Mist down into the valley where your town is situated and drowning everything and everybody in it, if you agree.'

There was a silence too long for my liking.

'So, what will be your answer?'

A moment on our language: I am addressing you in a language you understand, but all that I am recounting happened in our language, so I must give it a word or two. Elobian, the tongue ours is descended or derived from, is the language of the birds, fairies and dwarfs. But it has incorporated sounds from nature, snake hisses, pinetree rustles, the buzzing of bees and the lapping of ice. Still more, having been invaded so thoroughly and occupied so often, our country has taken words from many other languages and joined them on to ours. You should know, too, that the accent our tongues favour usually places emphasis on the first syllable of a word. This gives a poetic balance or a sad lilt to our speech, depending on how you listen. I will try to convey all this in my translation here.

'Old Frog,' said Hans Kansa, 'these are bad tidings indeed you bring. Why and how did fine young Walther buy it, and what is this wager of which you speak?'

'I smote Walther,' I said, not triumphantly but with private allure, 'gutted him with my tuskie-wuskies, and my wager is this: I shall spare the city on one condition. I desire not the Song Contest cup perched on its stupid hoof plinth.' I spat to emphasise the point. It seemed the thing to do, I don't know. 'I ask only for your daughter Lina, lovely Lina, to leave with me this very night as my wife and together we shall rule Owl Mist. Such a good honest wager; my word is my decree.'

Dunno why I said that last bit — it sounded a little wanky. To regain macho status, I snatched a tray of hot wine from a wooden market-stall and upended it into my gullet. Feeling mightily re-jigged and densely furred as a sniper's ghillie suit, I screamed for an answer. Look how the frog has been enchanted. Look how it moves.

Hans Kansa conferred with the guildsmen judges while sodden breaths were held. In their robes they moved like an opera chorus, as one, but each still unsure of the exact placement. Table bells were rung for extra slates — they were big on writing stuff down. I didn't dig writing much myself. Struck me as indulgent and time-wasting. Some aldermans' maces were banged on the stage, on to which they had clambered in disorder. Some woman began sweeping with a broomstick the doorway where the pigeons had been duelling. Tiny white feathers were all that remained now. My delicate amphibian flesh, stuck in the heat of the crowd, felt like it was being whisked in steam. Eyes itched. I needed a drink. So, before repairing to a local pubi, I spoke up again, this time in a cloying voice — boy was I a master of voices:

'You have until dawn to give me an answer. I am a reasonable man, and I am, as you well know, perfectly entitled to send the waters of Owl Mist down into the valley where your town is situated and drown everything and everybody in it. Walther told me: "The town is quite ready". Blame that tosspot if you've any complaints. I'll be in that pubi ...' I nodded toward the Town Hall, one corner of which had been converted into a faux-medieval imbibing den, '... er, awaiting your *yea*.'

It was a poor ending, yes, but I felt pretty clever. The plan was a good one. I couldn't see these loofah-brains seeing through it. But suddenly I had a different thought:

'And don't even think of evacuating the town. If I sense the slightest trick, the faintest whiff of duplicity, I will send the waters of Owl Mist down into the valley where your town is situated and drown everything and everybody in it, anyway. *Christ*.'

This was a mildly better ending. The guildsmen's daughters began wailing and huddling together. I had a sudden vision of them as a heap of tangled lesbians, hje hje, a clusterfuck for my benefit only of course. They would drop what they were doing upon my entrance and administer to my every tender whim. Hje. I strode across the square in my falcon-embossed boots feeling, and no doubt looking, like an intergalactic prince or vacationing demi-god.

I hadn't set flipper in a pubi in many months, or years (who knows really, what time is?). Some lambs, ponies and geese pottered between the tables. Well, I thought, this town's not all bad. I joined in the locals' games — a dominoes derivative played using coloured lacquer tiles, a form of billiards where the balls were struck using miniature croquet mallets instead of cues, an electric machine on which you could simulate butchering Germans and Russians, among others. I think they let me win, hje. As if *that* could sway a creature of my moral conviction. And everyone slopped back the local brew, a beer named Le Cock. No one dared attack me. Some certainly wanted to, but the reputation intimidates.

Soon the night was ending. Dawn began to coo. I rose and flipped my chair.

* * * *

Back at the Guildhall on Long Street, one of the very first roads in the town — indeed, not even I recall when the first cobbles were laid — and the first to link the Upper Town (the bit on the slope of the valley) to the port by way of the Lower Town, Veil Pognol, a goldsmith, spoke first:

'We must think rationally. Let no one yet panic. What are the facts? The bare facts. Please, Great Master Kansa, forgive me if I speak words that prickle you. We cannot fool The Frog. We cannot give him the girl Lina. We cannot evacuate the town, except by risking sooner death. We cannot stop the lake flooding and it is too late now to build flood defences. Why did we never do that, by the way?'

Bilthizar Korn, a pewterer, gloomily replied: 'Well, we didn't consider any watchman could be so stupid. How *could* they answer that the town was quite ready? They were picked for their unwavering answers even in the face of terrific distraction. And they were regularly re-evaluated too.'

'To be fair,' interjected Bearman Urtel, a soapmaker (widely regarded to be the guildsman with the lowest IQ — how did he *ever* make that much soap?), 'we are a peaceful singing people, unless we are invaded. We couldn't have been expected to foresee such depravity.'

'Shut the fuck up,' growled Fritz Thockner, a baker who, earlier that day, had become engaged to be married to Bearman Urtel's daughter Friska (and who was now regretting it: perhaps ignoring the hereditary qualities of idiocy was a mistake, particularly given the exploits of young Walther, he was thinking), 'you're not helping. Master Korn — what is this "terrific distraction" of which you speak?'

'I can answer that,' said the town clerk, Sixtus Beerknife, 'I devised the tests over sixty years ago. Although I'm never quite sure it was that long ago. Was it? Can you help, sir?' He addressed

29

Hans Kansa, at the head of the table. No reply was forthcoming, but Kansa's eyebrows dipped and surged at everyone in turn. Sixtus Beerknife continued: 'Oh well, never mind. It was a long time ago anyway. The tests broke over ninety-six per cent of applicants.. That's ... high. We were looking for the unflinchable, I guess. Tests started with simple torture. Freezing water, drowning simulation — appropriate, eh, given our predicament? Hje hje ...'

'Get *on* with it, Master Beerknife,' coughed Bearman Urtel, who was fingering his tankard as if he were about to crush it. Beerknife fluttered and continued:

'Sorry, yes. they came in threes. Generally. Matches, pliers, nails. Teeth, eyes, hair. Extremities, temperatures, animals. We went up in difficulty.'

'What the hell was the highest level?' This from Hans Foldtz, a coppersmith.

'Yes, that *was* rather good. A personal triumph if I say so myself. It was family members ...' Suddenly aware of the lengthening frowns around the table, he quickly added: 'The watchmen were well rewarded, never you worry. Not only in pay and prestige, although they certainly had their privileges — young ladies and so on ...' Realising his mistake, he mumbled an apology to Hans Kansa. 'They, er, deserved to be watchmen. They were the best of the best. Indeed, Walther was the best of the best. He earned it if anyone ever did. That's what I simply can't understand ...'

'Stop waffling and wait a second. We're not focussed. Master Vier Pognol was laying out the points. Please continue Master Pognol — you were on number six.' Everyone was surprised that Hans Kansa had spoken. His voice was cheaply brusque.

'Yes, indeed, sir. Thank you. Fool The Frog, give him the girl, evacuate the town, lake flooding, flood defences. These we cannot change. What *can* we change? Can we bargain? Not with a life, obviously — no girl will go to Owl Mist with that ... thing. What does he want? Can we do something for his lake? Can we ...' Vier Pognol saw that Hans Kansa had stood up. Everyone looked to him. Odd thoughts were showing on his face. His eyes made terrible shapes as huge tears, tears far too big for the eyes, tottered on the lower lids.

'Sir, are you all right?' asked August Mouser, a dyspeptic tailor.

Hans Kansa waved his right hand and arm wildly, then sat down again. Heavy in the body. Incredibly, the huge tears didn't drop. They merely kept growing, like two new and horrible eyes. He drank deeply and slammed the tankard down. Instantly, twelve footmen — one for each guildsman: as Alderman, Kansa had to finish his drink first — stepped forward and refilled all the tankards on the table from large elk-skinned jugs that were slung over their shoulders. Vier Pognol went on:

'Is there anything he desires, covets, more than Lina Kansa? Forgive me, sir.'

'We could offer to tear down those new blocks on the side of his lake,' spluttered Ilruch Eislunger, a grocer and a bisexual, 'after all, he did mention them in a venomous way. Or we could offer to give the whole place a makeover — what man could resist a full makeover for his lake ...?'

Pognol cut him off. 'This is useless. What do we know? There's Walther's betrayal — let his family name be excised from all documents at the Town Hall and elsewhere. Let there be no record of that treacherous lump or his significants — I want his parents picked up. *Wait!* Has he got a sister — no? *Damn.* That could conceivably have fixed the pickle we're in. Let's go back to the beginning ... Walther's betrayal ... and now the Old Frog's wager ...'

There was silence.

'... Sir —' Pognor addressed Hans Kansa directly. 'Sir, we appeal to you. We are at a loss. Speak to us, Great Master. Your wisdom has always won out. We beseech you.'

Eyes were moist by the time Hans Kansa spoke. For many minutes, or at least it seemed like many minutes but could have been more, or less, he twiddled tufts of beard. He tapped the huge table with reddened knuckles. Never looked up. Finally, he found his voice. 'We must ask the right questions to get the right answers,' he began, slowly. 'I have listened carefully. I have come up with two questions. First. Why did Walther give the wrong answer to the Frog's question?' Kanrid Nightingale (tinsmith), Cuntz Birdsong (furrier and Master Nightingale's distant cousin) and Jack Black

32

(stocking-weaver) shook their heads, not quite grasping the situation. But they were somewhat drunk. 'I merely advance an idea. What if he didn't?'

There was general hubbub. Several calls of 'we can't take that chance' went up, before Vier Pognol's voice carried over them in a wild, wavering baritone: 'He's right! Can't you see? The Old Frog is trying to trick us. Walther, as demonstrated by Master Sixtus Beerknife's methods — we need to talk on those later, however — would not have given the incorrect answer. His body was programmed not to.'

'Indeed. I believe this to be the case,' continued Hans Kansa, master builder, alderman of the Guild, head of the guildsmen and Lina's father. 'Even if you do not agree with myself and Master Pognol, you must acknowledge the logic behind our reasoning, and you must admit that, given this reasoning, it is a chance we must take. I am the only one who stands to lose in this. Not one citizen will die. But the third question must now be: How do we gain from this knowledge? If we need do nothing — the Old Frog cannot flood the town if the watchman gave the correct answer — then we must use this to our advantage. I do not enjoy the idea of my daughter acting as bait, but if we know he cannot flood the town, we could conceivably trap him in his deception. This would dissolve the curse of Owl Mist. Our town would be free at last. That snivelling little cunt could hurt us no more. And, if we are right, of course, let Walther be declared a hero. He shall be made an honorary guildsman.'

Oh, the poetry of our language. There was, after a fashion, much cheering and clashing of tankards. It was settled.

Poor Lina wouldn't know about all this of course. She'd think they'd given her to me, but she was just a girl and didn't matter all that much to the guildsmen, I guess, at least when they were in a celebratory mood. And that was their downfall, as you shall see.

* * * *

And oh, how my soul was cavorting, joyfulness upon joy, as they presented her to me, ribboned, on stage in front of the whole

33

wailing town. I noticed some odd glances between the guildsmen, but thought nothing of them, so exquisitely happy was I. I, me, happy. The Old Frog in thrall.

Hans Kansa made a speech along the lines of what a sacrifice he was making for the town — I yawned and jeered my way through that — then all twelve of them sang a close-harmony Song of Farewell — I practically dry-humped my way through *that*. Then the crowd parted and I made off with Lina over my horny shoulders, hje hje. Oh, the things I was looking forward to doing to her and making her do to me. As I bounded for Virtu Gate, hippety hop, gorgeous happy hop, ecstatic hop, she was nothing to heft in my arms, and I swear I heard her croak a little as we went. A fine start. This is what we want. My chinny chin scraped on her right hip as we went; her blonde head bobbed behind me. I had never felt like this. Hje hje. The smitheringales sang torch songs loudly from cream rooftops under a humid fruit sky.

And when we got to Owl Mist I showed her around in amazement, discovering the beauty of things as if for the first time. I told Lina the sorrowful history of my lake. I told her of the armies, from here and there. These guys in red, those guys in white or blue — they're always guys — but also of the fleeing refugees, the exiled, visiting dignitaries, aristocrats, sects, chanters, dancers, money-spinners, tall-tale tellers, dot com entrepreneurs, drunkards, fools and those who believe in gods. I told her of the misnaming of my lake, of the oils and the owls, the water cold and stylish, and the sound the leaves make as they brush the water. She trailed her fingers in it and listened. I told her that she was the oil aflame, and that her spirit would bolster the lake. I told her that all my misgivings and sadnesses were at an end.

And after we'd eaten — I caught a few fish and smoked them for her — I pointed to the apartment blocks on my east bank, and told her of her father's part in my life. How he'd 'contoured' the bank so that tenants in the blocks would find it pleasing ... How he'd ruined my friends', the birds', nests, how he let pollutants leak all over Owl Mist from his mechanical jungle. I pointed out the bi-chrome ravens on my rocky parts and the grassy island in my

middle. The bottleneck could wait. I said I didn't really hate her dad and would be happy to have him visit if it would make her happy. She nodded and said something about needing to sleep. I told her I'd have a good wash and then snuggle in beside her under the stars. I assured her of my good intentions, but I guess I sounded insincere.

And then when I got back from thoroughly scrubbing myself in slime, I found that she'd hanged herself with thick weeds from the viewing rail her father had put up on my western side.

I don't know if I've told you, but there is a strain of old men (to which I firmly belong) who, when confronted by collegiate and quite lovely pink female flesh, let their mouths run away with them. But they never act on it. It's talk. That's the point of us: we're raconteurs, wits, drunks and bores perhaps, but we keep you on your toes. Look at the quiet men. Now tell me who's more dangerous.

Of course I was far quicker than they expected. How could I not be? With their stubby human legs they waddled after me, but it took them hours to reach Owl Mist. I got there in a few minutes. Or at least it felt like a few minutes. Perhaps it was a few more than that. But by the time they got there, Lina was long dead.

The guildsmen raised such hell that I scrapped the curse myself. I didn't have the heart anymore. They could build bridges over me for all I cared, kill every bird here, dye all the ravens black as they are everywhere else, or so I hear. They wouldn't believe that I merely wanted a human, and particularly a female, touch for a couple of hours, and that I wasn't planning to ravage and abuse the poor girl. And of course, they took no responsibility for her death. They pricked me with spears and nipped me with scythes till I howled for them to leave.

* * * *

Epilogue

So, I hope you have learned something, boys and girls and those who don't identify as such. And, if your mum or dad is reading this to you at bedtime, get her to tell you about silence, or get him to tell you about noise. You'll notice things, little ones, little power. Reverse the two, in the morning perhaps. You're probably tired now, as I am, but then I am exceedingly old. I am so old you wouldn't believe it — who could? — and if you could, then you'd have an imagination that could sustain you through everything. Reverse them, when you wake up, your mum and dad. Make the men speak of silence and the women speak of noise and you will learn much. Mark this.

I have always held women in the highest possible regard, as you will know from reading what I have put down here, so you can see why I cannot forgive the men — and they are always men — who caused all this. Character suffers, or is it the other way round — characters suffer? I often look at reflections in my lake these days, and wonder which is the real. I see doubles. Tiny frogs have sprung up in large quantities on the island. I seem to be shrinking slowly. This is a mirror.

Owl Mist will have a less sorrowful history from now, hopefully. Boots will trample this place, but they'll be different: high-heeled, Ugg-ed, knee-high, winter, Gothic, work. Chipped optimistic stones will litter the lake's re-jigged recesses.

Come and see me some time. I'm still up here, and, so I've been told, look less like a frog these days and much more like a walrus. Indeed, my tuskie-wuskies are oft clicked by tourists with exceptional cameras. Don't worry, I don't mind. Why should I have quietude after what I have done?

I'm not at peace, despite what they all say. In fact I could do with a good snaffle of sexful girly flesh, hje hje — just wait till you grow up — you'll want it too, in some way or other. But I'm a peaceful being. Sad, old. Very old indeed — do you know? — me. Do you know me?

The guildsmen — Hans Kansa, Viel Pognol, Bilthizar Korn, Bearman Urtel, Fritz Thockner, Sixtus Beerknife, Hans Foldtz, August Mauser, Ilruch Eislunger, Kanrid Nightingale, Cuntz Birdsong and Jack Black, master builder, goldsmith, pewterer, soapmaker, baker, town clerk, coppersmith, tailor, grocer, tinsmith, furrier and stocking-weaver — well, they're still around too, if you ask in the town. Sometimes they'll even see you, if you ask nicely.

37

If they do, ask them to tell you the story you have just heard, or their version of it. I bet they won't. History swept away with a broomstick. They'll stay quiet. And they all lived woefully ever after. Good night.

* * * *

End Paper

A final word, for the adults. I went into the town recently — was it last spring? I don't recall. It could well have been. I am, after all, very old, and who understands time, when they bend their minds to it? — the Guildhall had been turned into a museum. *I know!* When did this happen? It surprised me, so I felt that a stroll inside was in order. I had some little trouble with payment — apparently they take strange Global Change these days, but they took a few fish in the end and I slopped around, looking at things.

I even got to sup a few Le Cocks in the adjoining bar. Turned out the barman was Jack Black, the stocking-weaver. He said he was singing more now, which I felt was a good thing. He seemed happy enough serving booze in the mini-pubi.

No one pays heed to me anymore, town-wise. In fact, the young people don't even know who I am. The old do, of course. They watch me sadly, or with tiredness, but without complaint.

Strangely, the museum has a model of me in it. Or at least I think it's supposed to be me. Beside it the text reads:

The Town That Will Never Be Completed

Every spring at some dark night an
old little grey man emerges from Lake
Owl Mist, goes downhill and reaching
the gates of the town, asks the
watchman: 'Has the town been
completed already?'

All the watchmen, however, have
been compelled by the court of law to
give the answer: 'No, the town is far

from ready. There is much to be built
yet and it will take a good many years
before everything is finished.'

The old man would shake his grizzled
head and mutter in frustration, turn
around and return to his lake. Should
the watchman accidentally reply that
the town is quite ready, the old man
would send the waters of
Owl Mist down into the valley where
the town is situated and drown
everything and everybody in it.

The model of me is terrible, all green and brown strips stuck to a
manikin. It portrays me as a merman or some such monster,
trapped in a ghillie suit made by disadvantaged kids. Never that
way, *please*.

I went up to the front desk and asked the girl — blonde,
ample-boobed, delicately creased chinny chin, green eyes, red
rucksack on the chair behind — if she'd ever actually met the Old
Frog. She said that it — it! — was just a legend and that I shouldn't
worry. I told her she was a thing to be amazed by and that she
should come out on a date with me to Owl Mist Lake. I used a
sensitive voice, slightly insolent at the top, but with rich undertones
of care. Boy, was I the master of voices. This is what I need. I must
stop waxing lyrical though. It never helps. I think I said that once
before. Did I? Who knows for sure?

Time is a ribbon.

Torrid Zone

Blinding cobalt blue. Ocean unwrinkled by wind or land. The horizon barely perceptible. No smell.

The Captain found that he was spending more and more time on the aft deck of the hydrojet, staring out to sea. This was the only deck from which any turbulence could be seen (the wake of the jet) and he found this refreshingly reassuring. With no landmarks, steadfast progress and a constant speed, it was good to know that they were still moving. He sat, mesmerised by the diverging ridges of displaced water, serene, remote. The pressurised hydrojet drive was enclosed entirely underwater, but, due to exemplary engineering, generated no noise: the wake was silent below. As there was no wind, the Captain could hear his own breathing, but nothing else. He dimly remembered reading somewhere of a room back on Earth, constructed centuries ago, to be entirely soundless, and that drove people insane if they remained in it for too long. An Anechoic chamber. That's what it was called! Thoughts from so long ago. Occasionally he imagined he could hear his sweat softly sizzling in the sun.

One could easily go insane in *this* weather, he considered, and never mind the Anechoic chamber. This bloody planet with no wind. Sailing ships would be useless. To be becalmed would indicate slow and awful madness and death. Thank goodness they were moving. Thank goodness they had the backup of Mothership, First Landing Camp, and the rest of the task force.

'Sunbathing again, Captain?'

Captain Will Palframan would have sat up, startled, but any movement at all was too much effort.

'Commander,' he said.

'Just to remind you that it's 9.8. Uplink at 10 and we have to have some sort of status check before lunch at 11.'

'9.8? Gosh, is it nearly almost noon already?' the Captain asked, standing a little too quickly. 'Thank you, Commander, I'll attend to it.' Blood coursed into his head and he slammed his eyes shut to avert a swoon.

'Are you all right sir?' the First Officer said.

'Yes,' replied the Captain, 'I'm fine. Yes. It's this weather. Nothing to do.'

He regarded the First Officer's pristine white uniform — crisp neat perfection — and felt slightly ashamed of himself. There were tasks to be concentrated on.

'Perhaps you should stay inside sir,' the First Officer offered, 'the Climate Control is functioning at 97 per cent. No discomfort at all.'

'You're a city boy aren't you?'

'Yes sir, brought up in one. My father was an aerospace engineer in Birmingham, sir.'

'Yes, well, quite,' said the Captain. 'I was born in the Fens, and I've always thought the inside unhealthy.'

'It's quite the opposite in the city, sir,' the First Officer continued as they walked towards the sliding doors into the body of the hydrojet, 'it's perfectly healthy of course both inside and outside on board ship. It's just that it's more comfortable inside. Less ... sticky.'

'Hmmm.' The Captain was thinking about how much he missed the song of the smitheringale, so sweetly and intricately bound up with childhood memories. Time was getting to him. This could become a problem if unchecked. 'Where are Ranagan and Baxter?'

'On port deck sir,' the First Officer said, before adding conspiratorially, 'fishing. *Sir.*'

'Fishing? *Christ.* They never seem to sweat,' he added, bitterly. 'In fact, neither do you.'

'Well sir, I stay inside if things get too hot. Ranagan's used to this sort of weather of course, and Baxter uses those Organosolvent body-temp regulants. Swears by them, as I understand.'

'Hmmm,' said the Captain again. They were now on the bridge, a semi-circular chamber with instruments and windows ranged round the curved wall that rose diagonally from the floor and into the ceiling, seamlessly. The Captain took his seat. 'How are we for time?'

'9.95,' the First Officer said, glancing at his chronometer.

'Fan-bloody-tastic.' The Captain moved his hand into the instrument panel's sensitive airspace and clicked his fingers. A floating holographic blue ball appeared in front of him, featureless other than a smear of brown near the Antarctic circle and a scrap of white near the equator. A glowing red cross marked the position of the hydrojet, a string of red dots its course. 'Good progress.'

An alarm sounded, signifying that it was 10.

The Captain sighed. 'Computer, establish communications uplink to Mothership.' The panel pinged. A white holographic rectangle appeared, faded to black, and the word Establishing came up on it in white. Presently this disappeared and was replaced by the eager face of the Expedition Communications Officer, Hanratty. He said: 'Good afternoon, sir.'

'Afternoon,' said the Captain. 'Just daily report, nothing exciting. I've uploaded the figures. The gist is that climate and conditions are constant, we're slightly ahead of schedule, the ship is purring like a fine tuned feline and provisions and morale etcetera are all fine. We'll reach the Torrid Zone in around eighty decs.'

'Copy. That's all good. Great,' the Communications Officer replied. 'Everyone up here will be pleased with that. Team 2 are ten decs behind schedule after engine issues. After all the problems on First Landing, it's good we are making up some time.'

'How is everything up there?' The Captain relaxed and gestured for a drink.

'Quiet. We're on the dark side at the moment. It feels strange. All we have to do is act as switchboard. Constant systems checks, inventories, diagnostics. There are only seven of us here now, in a ship built for thousands. It's bloody boring. I'm getting sick of Monopoly.'

The Captain laughed and clicked his fingers. 'Tell me about it. Not much activity here either I'm afraid. For an inhabited alien planet the scenery is bloody dull.'

'Yes, one would think that exploration and colonisation would be more interesting. But all the action so far has been at First Landing. Anyway, anything you're doing must be more interesting than what we're doing. Or what we're not doing. It looks lovely and hot down there.'

'Rather too hot, actually.' The Captain was twirling a little metal stick in his cup of tea.

'Funnily enough, it's pretty chilly up here,' ECO Hanratty said, 'Energy Conservation requires that we only heat the parts of the ship we use constantly, so all the hibernation and cargo decks are really cold, and the cold air wafts its way up here. It gets horribly draughty in the corridors. When we get back on the light side things'll warm up, I'm sure.'

'Right, I think that's it for today,' the Captain said, sourly. 'Nice talking with you.'

'Nice talking with you too. Mothership out.'

The rectangle blinked off and the Captain swivelled in his seat. He sat for a moment in obscure contemplation. He was not a large man and his eyes seemed sunken, a savage's eyes pasted onto a civilised, shaved and not unkindly face.

'Torrid Zone,' he breathed unhappily, 'Torrid Zone. Strange name for it. Sounds rather sleazy.'

'Torrid means intensely hot,' offered the First Officer, helpfully.

'This entire planet is one vast Torrid Zone. They should rename it. Torrid. Torriddu. Torridia. Welcome to *bloody* Torridia.'

'Torrid Zones are traditionally equatorial,' said the First Officer, 'the term might not be strictly applicable here.'

'Thank you *so* much,' said the Captain, unable to rouse himself to greater sarcasm. 'Has the temperature altered at all?'

Flinching a glance at a screen, the First Officer intoned: 'It has risen one half of one degree since we set out. The planet's erratic orbit and binary sun ...'

'... Combine to heat every inch of the planet's surface entirely evenly,' the Captain finished. 'Yes, I *got* it. Thus there is no wind. Precipitation is rare as the water in the atmosphere is stable and does not condense for reasons we do not understand, therefore there is no rain and no cloud, but everything is damp. Bloody *hell*. There is also no entertainment. I've read the bloody brochure. No wind and no rain.' He sat back, dejectedly.

'Except,' the First Officer said, 'in the Torrid Zone.' He managed a smile.

'Great. Bloody brilliant. Our mysterious little scrap of cloud. And everyone hopes ... an atoll?'

'Which, most likely, will be named after you.'

'That was in Mission Guidelines,' said the Captain, matter-of-factly, but inwardly brimming with pride. 'Don't worry, you'll get a geographical feature. You can choose any one you want, mountain, range, bay, cape, plain, basin, savannah, anything you want. A *parade* if you have to …'

'To the victor the spoils.'

'Well, there's only four in our crew so there should be more than enough to go around.'

'Small crew,' the First Officer nodded, 'the ship practically runs itself.'

'Yes,' said Captain Will Palframan, an ironic frown forming across his face. 'Sometimes I just wish they had put us in hibernation *until* the Torrid Zone. Perhaps they'll end up computerising everything, do away with humans in the exploration process altogether.' He sipped his tea. Wistful.

'I can't see that, sir,' rejoined the First Officer, 'I mean someone has to plant the flags and make the speeches.'

'I suppose you're right,' sighed the Captain. 'Okay. What's next? I think I'll change, go see what Baxter and Ranagan are up to and then may be a little lunch.'

'You're feeling better, sir?'

'You were absolutely right,' he said, dealing the First Officer a shoulder-clap, 'a bit of the old CC has done me the power of good.'

* * * *

Having changed, the Captain once again ventured outside, this time in protective headgear: a naval officer's peaked cap. He stepped out onto the port deck in a spirit of valour. Enthused and new. Vastly improved.

'Good afternoon,' said Science Officer Ranagan, without looking up from her deckchair, or even opening her eyes. Baxter, the Communications and Navigations Officer, snoozed lightly beside her. Their fishing lines trailed into the water, and the paraphernalia of fishing was strewn around their feet. Captain Palframan noted a plastic box containing three shiny metallic-green fish cadavers.

'Afternoon Lieutenant,' he said, 'nice sunbathing as per usual. No skin cancer to worry about on this planet. A productive morning, I see.'

'Yes sir,' replied Ranagan, 'they should go well for lunch and supper. This ocean is alive.'

'I'm glad you're having a good time. I'm finding it all a bit bloody dull if I'm honest.'

'Baxter too, I think,' she said, nudging Baxter awake.

'Have we caught ... Oh, Captain, I'm sorry, I didn't hear you come out on deck.'

'That's quite okay.' He walked over to the rail and squatted, fixing his eyes on the point where Ranagan's line met the water. Fresh fish had provided a pleasant alternative to the available reconstituted food, and although the Captain was initially wary about the possibilities of infection or food-poisoning, Ranagan had spent much of the first few days in her onboard lab providing myriad test results indicating that the fish were entirely safe to eat. She was the first to try cooking the fish; the texture was odd, tasting like fish should but with the toughness of meat. Having worked in a hotel kitchen before joining the fleet, Baxter took over, and his creations were sumptuous. In return, Ranagan taught him to fish, which gave him something to do. How she got all this equipment through the weight and bulk restrictions, the Captain had no idea, until he remembered that Science Officers were allowed to bring special personal equipment they considered important to the mission. She had cleverly considered the ocean planet a pleasing prospect and used her extended personal allowance to mix business with pleasure.

'I've just been talking with Mother,' the Captain said, standing up.

'Oh?' said Baxter, 'you should have called me.'

'Sorry, I didn't think. Nothing of import occurred.'

'What did Hanratty have to say for himself?' Baxter asked.

'He says he's getting bored, knocking around up there.'

'Yup. Sounds like Hanratty. What time is it?'

'It's 10.4,' said Ranagan.

'Well then, better do something about lunch,' said Baxter,

getting unsteadily to his feet and going inside the boat.

There was a long silence. The air pulsed, and the blue was blue, and the horizon was hardly there at all.

'How long now until we reach the Torrid Zone?' asked Ranagan.

'Eighty decs,' replied the Captain. 'Four days.'

* * * *

Two days of nothingness and unchanging progress. Then the Captain banned the consumption of fish. After a large fish supper the previous night, all four crew members had suffered virulent food-poisoning and spent an unpleasant night vomiting and consuming large quantities of pills.

The fish caught the next morning by Ranagan (Baxter said he never wanted to *see* another fish again, let alone cook one) showed high levels of organic toxins and certain anatomical deformities to internal organs. There were trace organic elements in the water which Ranagan said she had never seen before, and a higher microbe content. They were back on reconstituted food. And that was fine by the Captain.

Sitting on starboard deck that evening with a cool drink (pineapple flavour with a hint of lime, with little bits of Fake7 floating in it: his favourite), he stood up suddenly, sniffed several times, and ducked back inside. Ignoring how hard physical movements were.

The other three crew members were sitting in the communal room that served as mess and leisure area. They were playing Monopoly.

'Come outside for a moment,' he said, 'there's something going on. It's odd. I want to know if you can sense it too.'

They filed dutifully out onto the starboard deck.

'Well?'

'Bloody hell. Sniff. Inhale. *Smell.*'

'Ah, right.' They did. Sniffed with nostrils high.

'Can you smell it?' asked the Captain, anxiously.

'No,' Ranagan said.

'A little … fish,' said Baxter.

'Dead fish,' the First Officer said.

'Oh dear god …' gasped Baxter.

'It's just the remains of the food-poisoning,' said Ranagan, 'it hasn't entirely cleared up yet.'

'No, I can definitely smell it on the still air,' said the First Officer. 'How intriguing.'

'*Ohhmmnn,*' said Baxter, rushing back inside.

* * * *

The next morning the smell was tangible. Baxter had another bout of sickness which Ranagan zapped with drugs. Although recovered, he looked awful and didn't speak at all. Ranagan was increasingly worried by another rise in the residues in the water. More microbes and toxins were appearing hourly, there were fewer fish, and those that were caught displayed worrying tumours and deformities.

The First Officer spent most of the day struggling with the desalinisation and purification plant, which had developed a twenty per cent inefficiency and ceased to run the specified surplus.

At 10.2 the Captain delivered a lengthy, gloom-laden assessment of the previous 20 decs, listing in detail the problems that had arisen. However, no speed had been lost and time was still being made up. The Torrid Zone would be reached in just over 25 decs, at 15 the following day, early evening. Exploration would commence within 40 decs. Mission Control was happy.

They spent the next few half-decs downloading data. Reams and reams of technical data from the satellite probes for Baxter to ponder over, personal messages from family to the crew, more backup data. Final mission profiles, including details of prospecting, updating the originals with information from the islands they'd first landed on.

A vast planet with so little land … It was a bad joke. The first expedition had been very disappointing. An area less than western Europe, all cliffs and crags and mud, some scattered moss and a motley collection of uninteresting lichen. Already, the rest of the colonists were there, building a settlement, labs, an airstrip for shuttles. There were compensations: the mind-boggling quantities of fish that inhabited the oceans meant the planet could easily feed itself and export its way to economic viability. There were colossal iron and nickel reserves just offshore, promising prospects for tectonic development of more land. Perhaps there were even more hidden treasures in the immensely deep trenches that crosshatched the ocean floor, tenfold deeper than any on Earth.

The Captain was on the bridge, watching his parents on holiday in southern France. Drinking white wine in the sunshine, driving past vineyards and bleached hilltop villages. Baxter entered, drying his hands.

'Family?'

'Parents,' said the Captain. 'I'm seeing what they were up to a few years ago. Feeling better?'

'Yes, oh yes. Thank you, sir.' There was a pause. 'I've just been checking this satellite data ...'

'Hhmmm.' The data had been downloaded entirely raw, and the Captain had not been trained in interpretation, which was extremely difficult. To him it was just dozens of hexidecimalised numbers with occasional spiky graphs. 'Anything interesting?'

'You *bet*,' said Baxter, striding forward and palming some schematics onto the console. 'I've got a computer reticulating at the moment. There is an island, not big, probably part of a reef, with a surrounding shelf and various intriguing details. The satellite mainframe has even picked up a geographical feature: a large central valley.

'Right,' said the Captain, staring uncomprehendingly at the sheet of figures thrust in front of him. 'Baxter Valley? Baxter *Gorge*?'

'That's not all sir. No, not at all.'

'*Really*? I'm listening.' He wasn't, really. In truth, he considered this stuff all par for the course. It was a part of the job he hated: having to listen to the crews' yammering and moaning. Captaincy, in Will's mind, didn't run to promoting morale. He was a solitary soul, more given to savouring than flamboyance.

'Well, these satellites have their faults,' explained Baxter, 'especially early after launch, like the ones we're using here, but they're generally accurate when they're working. They *are* working. But I found a fault on one of the readouts. A sonar blip. Look at this.'

The Captain stared at the piece of paper in his hand. He wanted to understand, he really did. He scrunched up his forehead and even *pretended* to understand. But it was no good. All he could see was a sheet of figures arranged in a grid of groups of four. 'I'm sorry,' he coughed, 'you're going to have to explain this.'

'Well,' continued Baxter, handing him another sheet of identical figures, 'these are remote sonar soundings of a trench around 1200km from the island, one of the deepest trenches we've encountered. You see the figures are quite high. Anyway, there's a blip. I've highlighted it.'

The Captain located the highlighted number. It was the only

difference between the two sets. 'Yes, I see. It's a lot smaller,' he said, raising his eyebrows hopefully.

'Yes, but this difference disappeared on later satellite passes. Curious, eh? No?'

'Look, I'm sure you … Seismic disturbance perhaps?' He gave a shrug. 'That'll interest the tectonics experts I expect.'

'Yes,' mused Baxter. Then: '*What was that?*' His body had tensed and his gaze was fixed on the window.

The Captain sat up. 'What *is* it, Baxter?' No response. 'Is this about that bloody fish again? If you're going to chunder every-where, please go below …'

'Something hit the windscreen,' whispered Baxter.

'*What* hit the bloody windscreen?' shouted the Captain. 'Pull yourself together man, there's nothing out there above sea level. No birds, no rain, no wind, no bloody nothing.'

Baxter's face hardened; his eyes glassed over. He said: 'There's something out there,' and rushed from the bridge.

Swearing, Captain Palframan pursued his Communications and Navigations Officer out into the central corridor of the hydrojet, and then into the shorter corridor that led to the port deck exit.

'Wait!' he shouted, 'it was probably just one of Ranagan's pet pammplemoose got loose, like at First Landing …' Then he stepped onto the deck, where a wall of stench hit him. A stagger-ing world of decay. He gagged, and shielded his lower face with a sleeve before continuing. 'Oh, bloody hell …'

Baxter was standing at the fore of the deck, towel-over-mouth, staring up into the early evening sky.

'I had no idea it was getting this bad,' said the Captain. 'I was too CC-ed inside.'

'Look,' said Baxter. '*Look*. Up there.'

The Captain screwed up his eyes at the sky. The smell was so strong it was hard to believe it was invisible. His tear ducts began to give out and he retched. Up in the air in front of the hydrojet were a few floating black specks. They seemed to dive and swoop in the open air.

'Flies,' he coughed, reaching for the door, 'we must be near land.'

'They're monsters,' said Baxter, 'look at them. They're bigger than golfballs. Real monsters.'

'Flies,' the Captain spluttered. '*Flies*. Go and tell Ranagan, she'll have to know. We should try and catch one as a sample. I'll get in touch with First Landing, see if the naturalists there want us to do anything with them.' Then he wheeled in and ran for his quarters. He intended to take a long shower and then smoke a Fagscense, a legal and luckily regenerating cigarette that would obliterate all taste of the outside stink.

* * * *

The Captain had a long and tiresome talk with one of the naturalists back at Landing Camp, now an established town. She was more excited by the implications of the flies than by the flies themselves. Flies almost certainly indicated meat for them to feed on, and that indicated larger animals of some sort. On the First Landing isles, nothing more sophisticated than moss had been found above sea-level, and it had been thought that native fauna had not developed beyond the ocean-dwelling stage. The Captain used the opportunity to discover how the settlement was getting along, not having seen it for over a week. His crew had spent some time there while the hydrojet was being assembled, and the dwellings and facilities had looked rough. Now, it seemed, they were *comfortable*.

Messages took eighteen months to get back to Earth, so communication was an issue, but a message that the planet was ready for more settlers had been dispatched. It would take three years to get the acknowledgement message, and the settlers wouldn't arrive for many years after that. So there was plenty of time to get settled in.

Ranagan managed to capture one of the flies after a couple of decs prowling around on the fore of the ship with a reenforced butterfly net (part of the *standard* equipment, apparently) and disappeared into her lab to dissect it, pronto. Having killed it first, of course. The Captain shuddered, and readied himself for sleep.

Just before he turned in, as night shades enthused, Captain Will Palframan made a formal electronic note of a cloud, directly ahead on the horizon.

* * * *

The next morning he rose at 6.5 decs and went to the bridge, directly after washing and dressing, to take over from the First Officer. He was surprised to find it a lot darker than usual. There was almost no sunlight coming through the bridge windows.

'Good morning,' said the Captain, chipper, rousing. 'Cloudy?'

'Sir, it's astonishing, isn't it? We went under cloud cover at about 3 and it just didn't get light. I've had to seal the ship. The air outside has plunged below the quality threshold. And that's quite low. Organic toxins. It's like soup out there.'

The Captain stared out into the murk that surrounded the ship. It was a-dance with flies. 'How are we doing for time?' he asked, briskly.

'I'm afraid we've lost some, sir,' the First Officer said. 'The engine started to complain this morning, there's all sorts of gunk in the water. Ranagan's looking into it now. Probably literally.' The Captain shot him a disapproving glance. 'We'll hit land after 12. That's still good compared to the schedule we were working to at the outset of the mission, as we made up so much time earlier on … But I agree, it's a bit of a pain.'

'Mission Control won't mind, we're in their good books. Ranagan's up already, you say?'

'I don't think she slept at all, sir. She was working on that insect she caught at first, and since then she's been taking water samples regularly. She had to use breathing gear the last time. It's fetid out there, sir, to a dangerous extent.'

'Right,' said the Captain. 'Commander, go and get some sleep.'

'Thank you, sir,' said the First Officer, as he turned and left the bridge.

* * * *

After a lengthy midday briefing with both Mothership and First Landing, the Captain reconvened all the crew on the bridge for a final meeting before landfall. The isle was only a dec or so away. He cleared his throat, noisily. Then he cleared it again, aggressively.

Then he whistled to himself *hoooeeeeee* and shuffled some papers.

'The isle is surrounded by a wide reef and the water around it is relatively shallow,' he began. 'The reef is a sort of mesa on top of a great underwater mountain range, or so Baxter tells me.'

'That's right,' interjected Baxter, 'very, very interesting. Topographically speaking, of course.'

The Captain continued: 'Conditions out there are pretty nasty. We're going to have to use breathing apparatus and Encounter Suits for EVA. You all know the procedures, so here they are *again*. Hatches stay closed *unless* someone is in the process of going through them. Suits on at *all* times unless inside a green environment, that's all the chambers of the boat except the airlocks. Oxygen and seals checked *before* airlock engaged. *Christ*. Sorry, I mean ... Expeditions will consist of two or three people, no more, no less, and everyone has to know where everyone else is at all times. Record everything that happens out there for posterity and those long winter evenings ...'

'No winter on this planet,' said Ranagan, slapping down a pile of paper under the Captain's nose.

'Thank you so much, Ranagan. Mothership is working on a reason for the conditions we are experiencing down here, and First Landing is on it too. We're priority to them, which is good. Remember people, whatever problems we have will only be temporary. The terraformers and climatologists will be able to clear it up no problem. They're quite stumped about the specifics at the moment. Anyway, it certainly is *torrid* out there. You could stand spoons up in it. Conditions are playing hell with our instruments, so we're going to have to busk our way today until things get sorted out. So, any questions?'

'Would you be at all interested in my findings from overnight?' snapped Ranagan. She was a tall woman, solid yet gangly, and entirely unromantic. Bums met seats again. The Captain said, a trifle wearily:

'Of course, how rude of me. Science Officer Ranagan ...'

'The flies were interesting,' she said, 'but only in an academic sense. What is more pertinent to our mission is the nature of the water we are now travelling through. I took samples and it's ...

well, bizarre. It's a soup out there all right, packed with chemicals and degrading material. Rotting fish. A *lot* of fish have died here and are polluting the water on a massive scale. Look at this.'

Ranagan took a sealed petri-dish from her pocket and held it out for the other three crew members to see. Trapped inside was a bit of grey water packed with floating particles and little white specks.

'What are the little white specks?' the First Officer asked.

'Good question. So far as I can tell,' said Ranagan, 'they're bacteria. Bacteria so bloated they're visible to the naked human eye. They shouldn't really be alive, but they are, and thriving on the junk in the water. It's packed with all sorts of parasitic nasties. The air's alive with microbes as well. There aren't any fish anymore. They can't survive in these conditions. Plenty of flies though.'

'Dead fish. *Ohhmmmmm . . .*' said Baxter, running for the lavatory.

'Exactly,' she replied. 'Something has to be putting all this rotting fish-flesh into the water. I have no idea what could have done that. We have no idea what it is, so I suggest we stop now, retreat out of the Torrid Zone and await more data, may be from an overflight by copters. Or something.'

The Captain gathered himself. He shouldn't have to do this. He simply shouldn't have to do it and he didn't want to. But he was Captain and he was trained to be. 'About the mission? I'm sorry, Ranagan, I understand your concerns, but we're less than a dec away now. We can't stop now. I'll take it carefully. There's no need to rush. We can afford to be cautious. But we go on.'

A pause. Conflicted thoughts.

Suddenly, with a shrill warning beep, the hydrojet navigation computer announced:

ISLE WITHIN SHORT RANGE RADAR LIMIT

The ship altered course, slightly, toward its final goal.

* * * *

The unnamed isle was thin and oval, five times as long as it was wide. From the ocean its land rose steeply into a coastal range to the hydrojet's side, mirrored by a second range on the 'fat' side of the isle. Between these was a sharp V-shaped valley. Both ranges followed the entire length of the isle and dipped away into the sea.

In the murk and halflight, from the bridge windows, the coast appeared to glisten muddily, sloping up out of the noxious thick water that failed to lap as it should. A sickening shade of grey-brown.

The hydrojet sat motionless a few metres from the shore. Within the airlock, the Captain and Ranagan were suiting-up in order to set foot on the alien isle for the first time.

Once the suits were sealed they stepped out onto the starboard deck. An automatically-extending gangplank bridged the gap between ship and shore. Once the computer had established that the passage was stable, the Captain stepped forth bearing the flag. He stepped cautiously, aware that he was making history. The shore was spongy, saturated. Will took another step and plunged the flag into the ground.

This action pitched him forward. Luckily his helmet bounced off the surface.

Gathering himself. A few more steps. *Must be above and behind* for the photographs with the flag. He found his foothold and cleared his throat. 'I claim this island on behalf of the Greater European Association.' This was carefully recorded by several sets of cameras aboard the hydrojet, and by Ranagan's handheld, for undisputed verisimilitude. Press done, he regarded his planet and this new addition to the lands of his ancestry. 'We stand here as members of a glorious world …' he faltered, 'a world that, in its vision and scope of belief in that which is greater, has sent us forth to discover new worlds, new lands, for its people. This is, er, *Palframan Island*, and I welcome you to it as citizens of the universe. Is that enough Ranagan? Enough?'

Ranagan nodded and lowered her camera.

From where he stood the land curved gently away, shimmering in the haze. He bent to examine the terrain more closely. Beneath a layer of greasy slime encrustation it was grey and mushy, yet fibrous, like billions of stacked, wet, disintegrating newspapers. As he scratched the ground with his gloved hand, flies swarmed around the newly exposed areas, burrowing, flocking. Maggots oozed.

'Hell,' said Ranagan, suddenly. The Captain straightened up in alarm.

'What? What is it?'

'Hell,' Ranagan repeated, 'this is like hell. I would describe it as hell.'

'It is …' the Captain searched for appropriate words, '… alien. Very unlike anything I've seen before.' He felt strangely protective of the isle, his isle, despite its obvious absence of charm.

'No definitive flora of any kind,' said Ranagan, clambering further up the ridge. 'Quite a lot of fungus. Nothing spectacular. Ugh, these *flies*.'

The Captain moved on to item two on his agenda. Soil samples. He had a shovel strapped to his back. It was so light, made from an aluminium alloy, that he didn't even notice it was there. Moving well away from the flag, he popped a collapsible bucket into shape, before plunging the shovel into the ground and working up a hunk of it. It wasn't like any soil he recognised. It was spongy, interconnected, and there was something indefinably evil about it. Its oily greyness, the way it behaved. And the Captain was not a man much given to the use of such sentimental words as *evil*. The hunk he was working on tore itself from the ground with a foul ripping slurp. He dumped it in the bucket and sealed the lid carefully.

'We'll have to disinfect the bucket's exterior before we take it back on board,' said Ranagan, returning down the ridge. She looked like an astronaut in her bulky suit, and he realised that he must do too. Totally ridiculous. The air was perfectly safe everywhere else. Why was it so rank here? The Captain was almost taking it personally.

'What?' he said.

'Disinfect the outside of the bucket,' Ranagan said again. 'Not only will that stuff stink out the entire hydrojet if it gets loose, it'll probably infect the crew as well. I just took a reading and it's jumping with nasties. This place is a stud farm for the unpleasant.

They're breeding like smitheringales. I just saw a maggot the size of a human thumb. They appear to be feeding on the soil. It's very worrying.'

Leaving the bucket by the flag, they set off for a walk down the coast to the isle's eastern tip. The round journey would be just under five miles. With the marshy terrain it was heavy going, and not to mention the heat. The suits helped cloak out the worst of it, and they reduced humidity, but even then ...

'I can't see much of a market for those bloody holiday chalets I had planned,' mused the Captain gloomily, as he regarded his isle. Ranagan laughed, and her suit's respirator choked it into a rattle. 'The Costa Noxia.'

Landscape was fairly uniform. The coast curved away gently in front, the great ridge or range along the coast swept in an unbroken line up to their left. The sky was marbled grey. From many angles, the sea appeared sooty. Everywhere the same swampy gunk. The slime spread up to their knees, weighted down their boots, got into everything.

As they approached the tip of the isle they saw an awesome sight. They had been alerted by a bronchial roar from the other side of the range, and looked up to see the clouds over the central valley suddenly illuminated orange, and a spurt of flatulent flame leap over the top of the ridge.

'My *word*,' coughed the Captain, 'would you look at that? What do you reckon? Volcanic activity?'

'No,' Ranagan responded. She was working at her Environmental Supervision Unit, a sensor pad the size of an old mobile phone. From the 2090s say, or even earlier. 'The atmos here's got a lot of flammable gasses in it, but not in dangerous concentrations. It must be denser over the range, or may be it's spurting from the ground there. It might indicate fossil fuel deposits.'

'What do you think set it off?'

'I have no idea. ESU has noticed high static concentration in the atmosphere. Could have been an electrical spark. A little lightning strike.'

'Wow,' said the Captain, vigorously moving his chin to combat an uncomfortable itch on the side of his jaw. 'I hate these helmets.'

They moved on.

Eventually the landscape flattened very slightly and the height of the ridge appeared to be declining. Presently it became too marshy to continue, enveloping them to the hips and spreading out into the sea, a seamless morass. They turned back.

* * * *

It took a considerable amount of time to reenter the hydrojet. Hydrojets such as this one were designed with all sorts of situations in mind and were equipped with full decontamination apparatus. Upon entering the sealed lock system, the environment was saturated with a semi-liquid detergent gas before the Captain and Ranagan were doused in distilled water. This was repeated until the environment was clear. Then they removed the suits and proceeded into the hydrojet's interior. The decontaminant liquids were continually recycled for reuse.

Light was already fading by the 15 dec videoconference with Mothership and Mission Control. Quite a few people were linking in from First Landing, eager to hear about the size of the isle, several of whom the Captain had never seen before. The clouding in the Torrid Zone was so thick that survey satellites were having trouble with accurate information, and the discovery of the flies had piqued the interest of many of the scientists on the mission.

The Captain delivered a bland, toned-down version of the topography of the island, omitting the more strange details, and a perfunctory mission profile was delivered. There was then a general discussion about the island and what needed to be done, which the Captain found both irrelevant and dull. Having completed the bureaucracy and a light fishless supper, the crew retired for an early night.

* * * *

The following morning Baxter and the First Officer went out for a Reconnaissance over the ridge. The Captain was left with precisely nothing to do, and contented himself with reading and occasionally glancing through the window to see how the Away Team was getting on. The window from the bridge provided a fairly good view of the approach to the range the team had chosen, zig-zagging up its side, hitched together with polynylon cord, two hazy blobs against the slimy grey. At several stages they stopped to survey the view so far, or to take instrument readings, and soon they left the Captain's field of vision. If he felt it necessary, he could have listened in to their radio traffic, but that seemed uncomfortably like eavesdropping, something the Captain found distasteful. Besides, they would call if he was needed. He turned back to his reading.

After a short while Ranagan came on to the bridge and took a seat. 'Are the Commander and Baxter all right?' she asked.

'Fine,' replied the Captain, 'not a whimper from them all this time. Check. Med-telemetry fine. Everything appears to be fine.'

'What are they going to do when they reach the top of the ridge?' She was chewing a fingernail.

'It depends on the lie of the land. If there's an obvious path to take down into the valley they're permitted to follow it, if they radio in their progress. If not, they take recordings and come back and we consider action for this afternoon. Have you been looking at that soil sample?'

'Yes,' said Ranagan, 'for now. It's quite cumbersome keeping it isolated, so I'm restricted in the number of things I can do. It's horrible stuff … In some ways I'm reminded of peat by it, in others … Well, lard. It seems to have a corrupt cellular structure.'

'Cells?' the Captain asked, steepling his eyebrows. 'Organic material? In soil?'

'Well, yes, that's not very odd. All soil has decaying plants and animals in it. It's what makes it fertile. But this soil appears to have little or no mineral content, no sand, stones or gravel of any kind. Also, it's difficult to locate the source of the organic material. There are all sorts of living things in it, maggots, fungi, flies, germs, parasites, spores, but their decomposition pattern doesn't seem to fit. If there were some fish around here it might be easier to explain. But there aren't any inside the Torrid Zone.'

'Are you okay?' the Captain asked. Ranagan was looking stressed, he thought. She was pale and fidgety. Not normal behaviour. Certainly, he felt, outside the team-behaviour-protocol boundaries set down during psychological profiling back on Earth.

'I'm fine,' she said. 'But I'm not going to do any more tests. It gives me the creeps. I don't like not being able to answer the questions it asks. In fact, Captain, I would like to formally request that we leave the Torrid Zone as soon as possible. I'm not sure it's healthy.'

'Noted. I'll make that electronic asap, but we're perfectly safe inside the hydrojet,' rejoined the Captain. 'This tub's built to seal everything out. They considered the risk of alien infection when they were assembling the mission on Earth.'

Strange, how he needed to get the word *earth* in there somehow. It was unlikely he would ever see the planet of his birth again. Mothership was not designed with returning in mind. The settlement was permanent. The colonist ships that might be arriving later might be able to leave, but how long before they got here? If they ever made it. They cost a lot to build. If there was a change of government ... And even if it did all go according to plan, they were required to be here at least a year, then another eighteen months' hibernation. This wasn't simply another mission. It was a lifetime on this planet.

'Sir? *Captain.* You're daydreaming.' Ranagan reached out and rocked his shoulders, gently.

'*What?*'

'The Away Team is returning. Look.'

The two blobs were descending the ridge. Strangely, they weren't coming down the way they went up. Instead, they were sliding straight down the ridge, perpendicular with the coast. Straight down, faster and faster.

The Captain sat forward with a jolt. 'What are they *doing?*' he spat. 'They could damage their suits careening about like that.'

The speeding figures slowed gradually and reached the shore. He listened in. 'Captain —' 'Sir, get into your suit ...' The figures had reached the gangplank.

'*Yes?* What's happening? What's got into you?' asked Captain Will Palframan.

'Captain, get into your suit. You have to come up and see this,

63

sir,' Baxter gasped. They were over the gangplank now and standing on the fore of the ship, gazing urgently through the bridge window at them.

'Tell me what is going on. Away Team, you are not making any sense.'

'Please, just come and see,' pleaded Baxter, 'it's incredible. It explains everything.'

'Right. Here we go then.' He strode from the bridge thinking *perhaps my isle has some promise after all.*

* * * *

Outside, Baxter and the First Officer were back over the gangplank and waiting on the shore.

'What's this about?' the Captain demanded. 'It's not strictly speaking allowed, a Captain and First Officer on the same Away Team. This had better be good.'

'Bear with us, please,' said the First Officer. 'This is better than good. It's whole-heartedly astonishing.'

They started up the ridge at a steep angle, moving fast. It was hard toil. The land was smooth and greasy, slippery underfoot, and the respirators could hinder breathing as well as help it, if overloaded. The Captain was soon sweating heavily.

'The ridge isn't a ridge in the conventional sense,' Baxter was saying in between gasps, 'it slopes up on this side but doesn't on the other. It's more of an overhang, overhanging the valley, as is the ridge on the other side. Incredible. I don't want to spoil it for you.'

They struggled on. The cloud was thickening, it seemed, as they got higher. It swirled about them, gathering mist. The Captain thought of the mists of English mornings: this was of another quality. Not thicker, or more dangerous, but ... *evil.* That word again, stealing unbidden into his mind. The edge of the ridge was visible now, and it was not crisp, but mashed, ragged, like ripped-up strips of mattress. The flies were thick here. The Captain moved slowly forward.

'Careful sir,' said the First Officer, 'the edge isn't stable. It's treacherous.'

The Captain stared slowly down into the valley.

He immediately saw what Baxter had meant about the ridge. The opposite range was like a great wave, curving, ready to crash down. A truly mighty overhang, the colour of the land under it reddish-brown, quite different to the colour of land they had so far seen. Rising from the land were a rank of massive curved supports, each fifteen or twenty metres across at least, bleached white, evenly spaced. The floor of the valley, far below, was like a scene of hell. Ranagan had been right to use the word. Massive, churned purulent globes piled up on each other, red, pink and black, brown and grey, twisted tubes the size of trains, clouds of flies like smoke, buzzing cacophonously. The heaps were at least a hundred metres tall. Every now and then a rent would appear in these piled heaps of awfulness and vast quantities of gas would spew forth. It was reminiscent of ... It was ...

The Captain suddenly understood everything.

The smell, the flies, the corruption and pollution.

The isle and its terrible valley, the polished pillars on the opposite range.

He was staring into an open ribcage at the decaying entrails of a dead animal. A fish. This entire island was a colossal decomposing fish, rotting little by little over the centuries, sharing its poisons with the air and water, feasted on by a billion bugs. They were standing on a dead fish. A big bloody dead fish.

'My god,' gasped the Captain, 'it's ...' He fell silent. The implications of this were, well, frightening to say the least. Finally he managed to stutter: 'It must be over five miles long.'

'That's just what's exposed to the air,' said Baxter, looking distinctly green. 'The head and tail are underwater. It could be pushing ten miles.'

'But ... but ...' the Captain faltered, 'no animal that big could possibly survive! It would just die.' He felt like he was whining.

'Sure,' nodded Baxter, 'in the shallow ponds of Earth, but when an entire planet's your fishbowl.'

'We leave,' announced the Captain. 'We leave now and head straight back at full speed.'

'YES SIR,' said both Baxter and the First Officer, emphatically.

* * * *

They returned to their ship, decontaminated, and set off in a terrible rush, hurriedly explaining the situation to Ranagan while ignoring the midday hails from Mothership.

The hydrojet sped from the Torrid Zone at the highest speed it could be taken to. The four crew members went about their duties in shocked silence and only at 13, when the hails from Mothership and First Landing were getting desperate, did they finally acknowledge. Mothership was stunned. The scientists at First Landing descended into chaos, debating and shouting about the footage the crew downloaded to them.

'What do you suppose killed it?' asked the Captain that evening over dinner.

'It may have beached itself on that reef,' the First officer said. And after reflection added: 'like a whale on Earth. Couldn't get back underwater.'

'How many of them do you think there are?' asked Ranagan, 'down there in the ocean trenches.'

'No way of telling, I suppose,' said the First Officer. 'But now we're travelling at high speed, the motor's chewing through a fair old amount of water. We're generating a lot of wake, like nothing else on this planet.'

'You think ...?' the Captain tentatively put forward.

'Well,' replied the First Officer, 'when we humans detect something curious, indeed unprecedented in this case, we go and see what it is. I'd wager we're not the only ones.'

* * * *

40 decs of high-speed travel brought them safely out of the Torrid Zone and back toward First Landing. One third of the way back, an alarm sounded on the deck.

'Unnatural turbulence,' shouted Baxter, checking the console. 'Increasing.'

'Surface turbulence?' asked the Captain, hopefully, tapping the arms of his chair with all ten fingers.

'Negative, sir. Subsurface. Underwater.'

'What is it, Commander?'

'Radar reading impossible figures, sir,' said the First Officer, urgently. 'We're getting waves bouncing off something extremely large.'

'Is it,' enunciated the Captain, 'what I think it might be?'

'Correct size, sir. In fact, slightly bigger. Surfacing fast.'

More alarms began to sound.

'Where?' the Captain asked, panic now in his tone, '*where* is it surfacing?'

'Approximately half a kilometre away, sir, in clear view ...' The First Officer gasped: 'Coming up very very fast now ... Incredible.'

'Sir, we have to get away from here as quickly as possible,' Baxter said. 'It's vitally important.'

'We don't know it'll attack,' said the Captain, dubiously.

'No sir, but it's more dangerous than that. Something only slightly smaller than Manhattan island is about to break the surface at high speed. The waves it creates will destroy the hydrojet in a heartbeat.'

'You're right,' the Captain said, 'let's get away from here as fast as possible. Commander: take it away.'

'I think we can outrun it and get out in time,' said the First Officer. 'Engines are powering at A-1.'

Ranagan looked transfixed, radiant. 'It'll surface in just a couple of minutes,' she said. 'The aft deck should provide panoramic views of the spectacle.'

'Good point,' said the Captain, decisively, 'we can't miss this. It'll be worth the trip alone. Set all the cameras we have, and bring yours, Ranagan. Here we go.'

They regrouped on the aft deck with all the recording equipment. The hydrojet was fixed on autopilot travelling away from the surface point, which was visible as a far-off boiling circle of white foam and leaping waves. It was the most active they had yet seen the sea.

Then, to gasps, it surfaced. At first it looked like a silver bullet shooting from the water, growing longer and longer, its brilliant body climbing higher into the air like a column of steel, blindingly reflecting the sun. The Captain found it incomprehensible that what he was looking at was over twelve miles high.

Then, with a deafening *frish*, its whippy tail left the ocean and the fish flipped onto its side, crashing back into the water with the effect of a nuclear bomb. It spread a coronet of billions of cubic gallons of displaced liquid, a tsunami perhaps half-a-mile high, surging outwards at terrifying speed from the surface point.

As the crew retreated back inside to batten down the hatches, leaving a solitary expendable camera out there to relay a last few pictures, the Captain looked back at the spectacular farewell given to them by an inhabitant of the Torrid Zone.

Melania Hirsch and the Great Momentum

'addio, senza rancore'

'Fancy a shag?'
  'Gosh, couldn't you be a little more romantic?'
  'Okay. Do you like stars?'
  'Oooooh yes, I like stars very much.'
  'Good. Because I know a hotel that has three.'
  I dated Melania Hirsch for a year. She told me that I 'knew how to talk to women'. This was a good sign. It was terrifically good.

* * * *

Now, I don't know about you, but when I was a young man I resolved to diddle with the gentler sex as often as possible, so that when I came to the end, or just when prettiness had gone, I wouldn't be filled with regret and shuffle about muttering things like 'Why the hell didn't I?' and 'What the deuce was *wrong* with me?' However, as is common in life, I didn't recognise love when it came and sat on my face.

Melania was one of a steady line of ladies (indeed I noticed how they seemed to quite like the routine) to process through my unencumbered and lissom youth. Golly, was I a dreamboat? My ruddy brown brows curved over lilting green eyes. My bonce was topped by a blond thatch, the kind that looks rumpled, but expensively so. Boy, could I pull it off. It sometimes occurred to me that I dollied so many ladies because I secretly wanted to have sex with myself and could gauge how this might be by the reactions of as many bodies as possible. The only one worth having sex with seemed to be me. They couldn't *all* be wrong.

I diggled plump girls and bloodless anorexic ones, florid ones and hippyish ones, whores and marias, the creative and the accountant, the hatted and the skirted. The only ones I wouldn't touch were journalists: I mean, have you *ever?*

The only thing they had in common, except me of course, gloryboy, was dancing. What is it with girls and dancing? They *all* dig it — even those whom one might presume would not (given natural discrepancies: rotundity, an unsure sense of gravity ... one mustn't be vulgar) — really do. It's universal. A little like I was — universal: some here, some there — in those halcyon days.

I occasionally wonder if I donndled so many because I wanted to get to 'the one' faster. That's the romantic way of looking at it. But as I said (and although I didn't know it when we were physically together), over time I found myself thinking more and more about Melania Hirsch.

She was not necessarily my type, being somewhat shrewish, bossing, more features than flesh, more athlete than glamour model, more an ornate (and open to the public) cathedral than a Friends' Meeting House. Her gait was flat-footed, almost clumping, especially in the mornings, and she appeared to lean forwards, breast-led, when in a hurry. Her orgasms — and I always made sure she came first: what do you *take* me for? — were accompanied by a flustered whinny and much curving of the spine. Lavish care was taken. Yet when observed by many eyes, in a work meeting, say, or answering a question in front of the whole class, a charming delinquent gawp would appear and her hands would tense, the fingers splaying outwards. This was an expression of who she truly was, and no affectation.

But we only dated for a year and then parted, with the modern promises of friendship. I returned to my dongdingling ways, but recognised the absence. Mid-tumble I'd find myself thinking what her reaction would have been if I'd done this ('Oh yes, but of course') or that ('More, for sure, just on it there ...', 'Right ho ...') to her. It took some shine from the other girls to be honest. Perhaps I was getting old. And some of them may have noticed the preoccupation: I worried for my reputation. In short, my thoughts were abuzz with her. She made me chime.

And so it was that I resolved to win her back. The only problem was that she was by then partnering my cousin Daniel Albright (celebrity photographer — you may have heard of him). I had always got on well with all my cousins, but now instantly realised that Daniel was a complete and utter asshat.

Still, it was a TOTES AMAZEBALLS JUBILYMPIC YEAR according to *The Times* headline. I had bought my own house on Ball's Pond Road before the London Olympics began, and thus I thought it would be just the thing, a splendid, sterling and hunky-dory happening, if I threw a big party to celebrate this. I could invite everybody, and if perchance it afforded me an opportunity to re-seduce the glorious lump of gorgeosity that was Melania Hirsch, then all was to the good. I knew Daniel to be a drinker of the finest proportions — if he was flooded beyond understanding, then I knew I stood a good chance of working the magics on his lady. I knew she must still dig me. Why else would she be with my cousin if not to attempt to recapture some of our sexual stardust? I understood women.

So, the day after the closing Olympic ceremony, I got on the blower and on the computer — hell, I even posted a few friendly cards by snailmail — to my friends, and some acquaintances, to invite them to my sparking new abode/loveshack.

* * * *

'When we get back I want a blowjob.'

'Couldn't you be a little more romantic?'

'Okay. When we get back I want a blowjob next to a candle.'

Gosh, was Melania a considerate bird. Death would come for us all, but I realised she was one of the Immortals.

* * * *

Come the big night, everyone was having a grand time. I had the film *Barbarella* projected, on loop, onto the living room wall. Drinks were multi-chrome and had tiny umbrellas in them. Daniel was apparently coming with his brother Josh, a doctor, and Melania was to arrive later. As I predicted, things were proving auspicious. Ah, it was all to the good. Suddenly the doorbell went. It didn't chime, oh no: it *played* Wagner's *Ride Of the Valkyries*. A computer-rendered recording, sure, but I felt a certain impression was formed. And there was Daniel, leering horribly.

'Where's Josh?' I said. I didn't think it too much to ask.

'Sorry old chum. He was with me earlier. I think. We got a cab. Perhaps he fell out on the way. Sorry, old boy.'

Ha. He was already somewhat booze-zoned. Again: there it was.

Auspicious. I wasn't worried about Josh. He'd turn up. Doctors usually do, cocktail flu a common excuse. No one ever notices when doctors do everything right. There's no bright-spot analysis.

Daniel rushed off to tell obscene jokes and make half-hearted passes at everyone present before throwing up a bellyful of foam in the garden. It was predictable, but you couldn't dislike Dan (except for me: I had reason) — he had intelligence and charm, and weaknesses the opposite sex were attracted to curing. Of course, he was a photographer too, and women sensed this. Even the disproportionate or lop-sided woman can sense a photographer, and it stimulates their desire to curve, to fawn. Distilled versions of the life forces.

The party was thus far filled with bohemian types. Three of my ex-girlfriends were there — Elloway, Pikaia and Arlesienne — although none of them knew each other. To be honest, I was hoping to give it to one or other of them like a steam train that night if things didn't go well with Mel. Sweet chiming Mel. I must have been an extraordinary lover, a tremendous talent in the sack, riding them like Seabiscuit. And I was still *persona grata* with them all, naturally. *Carpe noctem.*

These were the thoughts going through my head as I opened the door to more people. Drink constantly refreshed. Oft congratulated on my new house. On my elephant, sorry, *in my element*, a king, surrounded by the plosive sneezes of cans being opened, wan evening light streaming through big picture windows.

Eventually Melania Hirsch, with a *frish*, arrived and announced, wonderfully (or so I thought): 'Sometimes one simply *has* to dress like this.'

Well no, one doesn't, but I was frankly glad she had. She was wrapped in what resembled a roll of muslin — coarse to the eye, yet giving to the touch. Patterned with vines and leaves, ribs pulsed beneath. It was the most erotic piece of material I had ever beheld.

However, things didn't get off to the best start. After imbibing a few more beverages and copiously tonguing Mel, Daniel slunk off back into the gloomy thicket of the garden and curled up beneath a smallish Rhododendron, cigar smouldering into threadbare grass. Then, scarcely twenty minutes later, I discovered Melania sloppily blowing my friend Will Palframan (who worked behind the counter of my local chicken takeaway), on the ladder to the loft. I recalled this quirk of hers — while hardly racist (she'd had her fair share of brothers) she much preferred to suck black cock than fuck it. It was an aesthetic thing apparently, to do with the 'sturdily-veined upward curve of the glistening shaft'. Well, I just don't know anymore.

'Jesus Christ!' I yelped, 'there are people here — it's a party! Couldn't you guys be a *little* more discreet?'

Will began to wave his arms as if he were conducting a Justin Bieber song, but Melania smiled that helpless and irresistible smile and as she spoke my heart became bubblebath gloop. She purred: 'Oh darling, don't be jealous like that. Me and Will here — it *is* Will, no?' (That *no* was so goddamn sexy.) 'Me and Will mean nothing. It's just a batshit party, sweetheart.'

Feeling somewhat desultory, I hobbled off to raise my spirits. However, a brief conversation with Elloway, a Ghanaian/Scottish beauty queen/concert pianist hybrid I dated six months earlier, that at first seemed to be doing the trick, ended up further lowering my spirits. It went something like this:

'Darling, are you enjoying the party? Thanks so much for coming, by the way. You're looking wonderful, ravishing, fulsome.'

'I know, but you know I always do, darling,' she condescended, leaning in for an exaggerated air-kiss. *Poof.*

'Do you like the place? What I've done with it? I mean, it's a work-in-progress, sure, but it, *I*, show sincere potential, no?' I noticed her grimace, but ploughed on. 'Now, back when we dated perhaps you could have argued that my interior design sense left something to be desired …'

'Are you coming on to me? I very much hope *not*,' she replied, aggressively rubbing the stem of her wine glass (*red* wine too — what would that do to the carpets? Or paintwork? Or even clothes?).

'Indeed not …' I rose deftly to the defence, explaining how I had had the place decorated and furnished to pamper the eyes and palette, not to mention the nose. I discoured on 'the solid silence of the rugs' and the 'musculature of the large front bush', a *Laurus nobilis*, I believed it to be. Elloway seemed disinterested, but on I flowed about the camouflaged CCTV cameras in the drive that followed you with disdain as you passed by, about the pitch-pine raked cellar floors, about the smitheringale-decorated personal bar (I *know*), until it could be ignored no longer …

'Am I boring you?' I asked, not forcefully but with straight eyebrows, 'okay then. I'll change the subject. What do you do now? How's work? Still playing and performing? Or are pageants more where things are at these days?'

Elloway didn't take this well. Her sulphur-coloured lips parted, a-snarl. She was apparently named after some wife in a fairytale. Enjoying the chaos, I didn't miss a beat: 'Because I figured the modelling would be the future. Talent in looks rather than fingering, so to speak, penisitcally, sorry, pianistically. Say, do you dance? I think that's the new Why Doesn't She Just hit playing downstairs. Fancy joining me in some slut-drops?'

'No one expects the Spanish Armada,' she hissed. A moment later the warm wine hit me.

* * * *

'I was not *drunk.*'

'*Good god*, old chap — you kept asking my cat why he killed Mahmood.'

'Oh god, seriously? What did Mel say? How am I ever going to live this down?'

'She didn't even seem perturbed, dude. I wouldn't worry. I reckon she's a keeper.'

* * * *

Suddenly, from below, ragged cries erupted. I confess to being a little under par, but sobered at the joyless noise. Making for the stairs, I tripped over a rug and came a cropper on the landing. My nose crunched on the balustrade. Adding to the red wine, blood began to seep bashfully from both nostrils.

'He's scaling the facade!', 'He's shimmying up the drainpipe!' and 'He's going to die!' were three exclamations I distinguished as, holding my nose to staunch the flow, I wheeled on my heels.

Springing through a bedroom door and finding a front window was with me the work of a moment.

I was confronted by Josh Albright's chin on the windowsill and one of his hands waving urgently. The eyes were a tad crazed. I thrust the window up and bowled Josh into the room.

'You're bleeding,' he gasped as he landed on his knees, right in the centre of my stomach.

'You don't say,' I spluttered. 'What the spindleshanks are you doing climbing my house? What of the neighbours? My reputation?'

'Soz, cuz, it's just no one was answering the doorbell. It makes a hideous noise by the way. I wouldn't worry about your reputation. I must say, as a doctor ...' I tuned out. There may have been detectable sarcasm in his tone, but it was the past. He felt crowded out of things. I didn't push. And wonderfully, the boozy ebb and flow of shared evenings began to reassert itself. Grupero music (influenced by the norteno, cumbia and ranchero styles: *Tesco* in street parlance) was burbling from my hidden speakers.

Fast-forward an hour. With Josh now sloshedly watching *Barbarella* (on loop, if you recall), and Daniel still pretending to be an armadillo outside, I felt all social paths opening up, and made a beeline for Pikaia, who was standing alone in the kitchen. Sharpish, things were looking good.

I had briefly lived with Pikaia when I was a student. Her namesake was a two-inch worm-like creature named *Pikaia gracilens*, that was itself named after a mountain near the Canadian Rockies where it was found, and for the sinuousness (almost sexiness) of its body. The importance of this creature stems from the fact that it was one of the oldest recorded vertebrates and the only one, out of millions of other life forms, to survive the Cambrian period. The Big Extinction. Thus, with the lack of other provable examples, and against all the odds, this tiny prototype's survival led to the development of the human species, and every race. Boy, was she something.

She was from Ohio, and my first impressions had been of her smoking a joint between question-mark lampposts and blowing beams of smoke from her eyeballs at the turn of the 21st century.

Then I got to know her and the great tradition of glittering American sadness, somehow perfectly captured by wearing boot-cut 501 jeans and smoking French cigarettes while affecting a lesbian air. Through her, I also got to know that 'liberated' chicks thought nought of shitting in front of their boyfriends. Pikaia would take a dump like shoes falling out of a loft while I was brushing my teeth in the same bathroom — and by our second date! *The horror.* But I liked the carelessness and absolutely enormous eyebrows. Refulgent. I recall that she briefly toyed with becoming a doctor to find a 'cure', but then didn't, instead opting for a sellotape then wax-based one. I reckoned it a turning point in her history and probably why she went on to become a member of parliament, namely MP for Hounslow South.

'Darling, are you enjoying the party?' I asked. 'Thanks so much for coming by the way. You're looking wonderful, ravishing, fulsome.'

'Yes, thank you for noticing. It doesn't buy you brownie points though, I'll have you know. And I'm not talking of druggy biscuits when I say brownies, rather using an English expression, or cliché, to make my point.'

'Yes of course. You know the old joke. You can't become a scout till you've eaten a brownie and all that?'

Pikaia raised her sculpted/tattooed eyebrows quizzically, a rearrangement that somehow involved every muscle in the lower face.

'No? Not in your US lexicon? *Christ* ...'

She was unimpressed. Her lovely head inclined millimeterically toward her pint-glass of Guinness — black, and foul to clean out, I was fairly sure, of carpets, paintwork and fabrics ...

'No, I do not know "that joke" as you put it, but it strikes me as misogynistic, cruel, anti-social and stupid.'

'Gosh,' I stammered, 'that wasn't what I meant at all ...'

But, with relief as palpable as ejaculation, I realised I'd misread her. Pikaia wasn't about to toss her drink in my face. She pulled a slender croc-skin clutch bag round her body and opened it. Then she withdrew a palm-sized laminated card and pressed it on me with a careful:

'My darling, my old darling, I worry for you. I care more than you realise. And I see that you are suffering ...'

'... ? ...'

'... and in pain. Let me help you. Here. Read this.'

Perplexedly, I lifted it to my eyes. Then the horrible truth hit me. I read:

> Do not take part in any of these components of Satan's Spiritual Structure.* They are doorways to demonic possession.

Eastern religions	Divination	Marihuana & Pot parties
Yoga	Meditation	LSD/shrooms
Freemasonry	Vegetarianism	Video games
Illuminati	Lycanthropy	Harry Potter
New Age religions	Postmodernism	Dungeons & Dragons
Church of Satan	Backmasking	Halloween
Scientology	Astral-projection	Fornication
Rosicrucianism	Necromancy	Skull & Bones
Astrology	Re-birthing	Rock music
Tarot cards	Kabbalah	Heavy metal
Ouija boards	LOTR	Burning man
Remote viewing	Fire walking	Twilight films
Palmistry	Levitation	Raves & XTC
Voodoo	Alt "comix"	Goth culture
Earth Worship	Vampirism	Cyberpunk culture
Wicca	Trilateralism	

*Eph. 6: 12 & Deut. 18: 9 - 12

It's fair to say my soul harrowed. I'd had this kind of illiterate douchecopterish booboo through my irritated letterbox before, as had nearly everyone else in London. I knew the score. What the scratchstink is wrong with everyone tonight? I thought. What *is* it with them? But I said:

'Er, thanks. There're quite a few mistakes, er, errors in spelling etcetera on your lovely, er, handout, circular, er ...' I was hesitant, you see, because I wasn't at all sure how she'd take even this mild criticism.

But again I was relieved. Pikaia shrugged (a rich deliberate movement — I was momentarily reminded of her shitting in front of me) and said:

'My friend Harvest checks all that, I am merely the vessel.'

Then I made my mistake. Much too quickly I said:

'*Harvest?* You know someone called Harvest? As in *Harvest Moon*, the Bedlam song? Ho, that cracks me up. And what on earth could possibly be harmful about vegetarianism, apart from the evident boredom? Even in prehistoric times veggie dinos were boring. The carnivores had more chutzpah, put themselves about more, exhibited charisma. Most of the rest of the stuff I'm with you on. Well, not really, but I can see where it's coming from. But if the mistakes aren't mistakes, if Harvest is a top sub-editor, say, or award-winning novelist, if you want mari*hu*ana for example ...' (here I pointed to the relevant bit of card, perhaps a little too close to her nose) '... then you need to put *sic* after it. As in *sic erat scriptum*, literally *thus was it written*. Yeah, and ...' (even I admit that my tone was portentous) '... here you need a *sic* too. *Sic, sic, sic* in fact!'

'How dare you call me sick after the things you made me do under the sheets?' screeched Pikaia, 'and after I came to your party in all good and holy faith, despite how you treated me way back when?'

Trying not to smile at the Americanism, it was then that I recalled that I had in fact cheated on her with a stripper named Minnie Mirror (though I suspect that may have been her working name) and then broadly suggested a threesome. I decided to deny the whole thing, a course of action that sometimes, unbelievably, worked.

'What could you possibly mean ...' I began, but then her Guinness hit me. I was not at my best, to be fair, by this point. And as if things couldn't get any worse, my revellers had begun singing *en masse* the new song *Needles* by the teenybopper band Why Doesn't She Just, with its foul offensive lyrics:

I don't trust anything that bleeds for five days and doesn't die
That is fucked in oh-oh-oh so many ways and why?

Someone must have slipped it into the drive. I hated everything Why Doesn't She Just had ever released — and their releases were everywhere. Without being negative, the band (although consistently riding high in the upper echelons of the charts) had been rather sour of late, their hits including *Give Us A Payrise* (about a mutual groupie who'd given them all herpes) and *Can I Remind You Of Your Love* (about a record industry rumble concerning royalties). And no, I haven't made a mistake — they really were that way around.

My eyes smarted. Groping wildly after the departing xylophone of Pikaia's spine, I slipped on some spilled lemon juice. The corner of the open oven door welcomed my skull with an internal clunk. I came to, dazedly cradled by some guests (who *are* you?), a clump of sodden red kitchen-towel pressed to my festive head.

'What happened?'

'Looks like you got plonked by your ex, you dreamy fool,' said Josh, the doctor, who had by now sobered up — probably at the sight of blood — and was greedily eyeing the bottle of Tunguska Vodka my left hand was inexplicably gripping.

'Where is she?' I asked. 'And stop dabbing at me — even you, doc. Cease. Step down.'

Josh conjectured: 'She may have left. We're unsure as to the situation. But I want a Martini chaser down here right now, followed by a Courvoisier drip ...'

Many things occurred to me to do. But in the end I did what anyone would have done. I punched the malignant fuck on the nose. Josh fell back and coughed with the delay of the well-brandy-ed. A virile cough. I hated it.

'So? Where *is* she? Not Pikaia you dunderheaded-douchecopter, Melania. Mel Hirsch.'

'What did you hit me for?'

'Christ cuz,' I said, handing him the vodka bottle as I stood. 'At least don't let them fuck with my music system. *Put something on.*'

'You want me to dress up? Or dress someone else up? *You?* Oh god, dude ...'

'No, put some MUSIC on the FUCKING SYSTEM!'

'She slept with her sister last night.'

'Well that sounds okay. Probably just shared a bed. They're sisters. I'm sure it's nothing to worry about.'

'No, you don't understand. *I* slept with her sister last night. She's such a liar.'

Boy, why did I ever dare treat an insolent goddess like Melania Hirsch so?

* * * *

People dream of what they might have done if they'd been loved — nothing cures that. We all feel it. It's universal. Like girls and dancing. Or my winkle in those dhondying times on the club scene some years ago. Did I mention that before?

So I picked myself up, poured a pint of icy cider and headed for upstairs. Thanks be to Josh, for the music now pumping was The International Colouring Scene. A fine band, if a tad anaemic …

By this point — it must have been well past bedtime — I felt that I needed Melania deeply and nothing else would do. Behind me Josh said:

'So why are you looking for Mel? And how do you feel?'

'Fine, thank you. I'm looking for her … Say, is your brother still comatose in my shrubbery?' I asked, pausing on the stairs.

'Oh no, last time I saw him he was photographing your guests in what he called *comic* poses. I would say more …*s uggestive ones.*'

'Jesus. Look cuz, I have to be honest,' I said, feeling used and wretched and not turning to look him in the bonce, 'I've been doing a lot of thinking since buying this place. Isn't it beautiful by the way? Don't you love the remote-controlled sloping sky windows with the rain sensors, the retractable garden lights that make that lightsabre *ziooong* as they come up …'

Josh cleared his throat, indulgently not abruptly.

'Sorry, I'm getting off topic. As I was saying, since I got this place, *settled down* so they say, so to speak, ahem, I've been doing much thinking. And I've realised something totally important. I've realised that I'm simply in love. Deeply in love. With Melania Hirsch.'

'WHAT???' The roar came from our legs. Josh and I turned to Daniel's face pressed between my firefly-carved handrail spindles. Well, it certainly looked like curtains for me, but I took off upstairs at as good a trot as I could muster under the circumstances.

Dan bounded after me with a low-slung, simian gait. Three cameras swinging wild round his neck. His brother stood in the way, and even though I doubted he'd last long, the distraction might just buy me some precious seconds. Of course I recognised the effect that the splendid wedge of splendiferousness that was Mel could have upon a man (look at me) and so I wasn't about to let Dan Albright, celebrity photographer — you may have heard of him — my cousin, and *kickboxing champion,* catch me if I could possibly help it. Just thinking about her, even when in terror and mid-flight, made me realise I had an erection bubbling away. Okay, only half-mast, but it still goes to show what a girl she was. No?

'Meeeee*eeeee*el,' I screamed as I ran, or ran as well as I could with that semi. I reached the top landing but still she was nowhere around. Suddenly the bedroom door to my right opened and disgorged Arlesienne, the third girl in my sexual history to be at the party, alongside Elloway and Pikaia. Her blouse, patterned with vines and leaves (I noticed) was three-quarters open, right to the belly button, and her hair way oddly dishevelled. Wait. She was *never* dishevelled.

'Arlesienne,' I gasped, 'you've got to help me. There's a furious boyfriend after me and he just happens to be a karate champion.'

'Well this sounds familiar,' she smiled.

'By the way,' I said, 'thanks so much for coming tonight to my little shindig. You're looking wonderful, ravishing, fulsome.'

'Thanks babe.' She was Australian you see: that's the kind of stuff they say. 'Come with me.' And taking me by the hand, she twirled me into the bedroom she'd just emerged from as Dan's footfalls loomed. Holding a delicate finger to her lips, she motioned for me to get into a large cupboard in the corner. I flashed her an *it's hopeless* expression, but she mouthed *trust me*. Getting into

the big dark thing was with me the work of a moment. As I closed
the doors, Arlesienne flung the window open.

* * * *

'I've got one for you,' whispered Melania Hirsch, blonde, moral
and perfect. 'Why are men supposed to prefer to marry virgins?'
　　'Go on then.'
　　'Because they can't stand criticism ...'
　　Lord, I loved that woman.
　　'You fill me up,' she said. 'Now.'

* * * *

Wait a second — I just said that. *Go on then.* Actually said it, dear reader. This just happened! This was no memory — in the cupboard I felt her tongue on my cheek. I instantly almost doubled-up in lust, but caught myself before I head-butted the door, as Dan rushed into the room shouting:

'Where the spandleshinks is that runty shit?'

Mel placed her hand across my mouth. It was warmly moist and smelled of geraniums. I sometimes think I lack human impulses, especially the hopeless ones, the warm, the cuddly.

But at that moment you could have tweaked me with a feather and watched me fly. We heard Arlesienne say:

'Why *hello*, big brute, who are you talking about? Come here. There, there ...' I could imagine her pulling him to her unclasped bosom.

'Our goddamn host. Where is he? I am inspirited with fury,' thundered Dan.

'Da*aa*rling, he went out of the window,' replied Arlesienne, 'look at this enormous drainpipe. Solid steel. Swung straight down that. Never seen him move so fast. But then he did say something about you and Taekwondo.'

'Kickboxing,' scoffed Dan, 'a far superior discipline. He went down *that?*'

'What are you doing in here?' I croaked to Mel.

'Do you really need to know? I'm here with you now.'

'Were you ...? Were you and Arlesienne? Is *that* why she was dishevelled? Australian girls of her age are never dishevelled abroad. *Christ*, Mel ...'

'Sshhh.'

The music was now belly-dancer-shimmering-esque and was seriously adding to my jitters, sweats, palpitations, arrhythmia. There were speakers in every room. Mel began stroking my chest. She probably intended this to soothe, but I was so in love that her merest touch might bring me off. Christ, it would be like bucking the slobbering donkey during the opening credits of a porn film, just for the dashed *atmosphere*. But then, in that cupboard, that's what there was — atmosphere. Arlesienne said:

'Ah, sweetie, look at me. Only at me. Yes, that's good. *Me.* Now

85

watch. Ooh. You like?' The Oz accent rose and fell.

'What's going on? Is she seducing him? Do we run when they get stuck in?' sniffed Melania. But I was sensing a plan. Arlesienne had always been a cunning lady.

Her name came from a short story, *L'Arlésienne*. Set in Provence, the girl from the Arles is loved by a young guy, Fréderi who goes mad upon discovering her infidelity prior to their wedding day. He commits suicide. The story never really caught on. Too Puritan may be, for France, but obviously not for me. Interestingly, because the title character is never shown in the play, Arlésienne is now used, in French, to describe a person who is prominently (and sometimes voluntarily) absent from a place or a situation where they ought to show up.

She was the friend of a friend on various social media. I sent a message: Hey, I had to add you because I can't keep wanking over the picture of a girl I haven't met. She was understandably flattered. A top chick, if lacking the Hirsch sorcery.

'Listen,' I whispered to Mel, 'I may be wrong, but I think Arlesienne's getting him to *photograph* her. It's brilliant — I'd never have thought of it ...'

Meanwhile the band I loathe more than any other, Why Doesn't She Just?, had come on below our feet, this time with their forthcoming Christmas single *Twinkle Twinkle Little Whore, Close Your Legs They're Not A Door*. I almost sobbed with frustration.

'I want you by the window. Ooo. Look more like that. Yes. Now show me muscles and bend over ...'

'WAIT!!!' This was Dan. 'What was that noise? Is he hiding in that cupboard? The turd. I'll rip him apart. Step aside, lady ...'

'Okay,' said Arlesienne, 'bye.'

I yonked Mel from the cupboard ('*Andiamo*, love,' I remember her saying) and made for the door. Her hand was in mine and we were almost out of the room ... when the door flew inwards and hit me perfectly in the mouth.

* * * *

A woman without curves is like a road without bends. You may get to your destination quicker, but the ride is boring as hell.

* * * *

Well golly, gosh, and what a lark. I surfaced and instantly understood the weird alchemy that turns misery to humour. Enough of this sexual kindergarten, I thought, pulling myself upright. Unfortunately, the blood from my hard-on immediately reentered my system and, momentarily dazed, I fell down again. The air was pressured, parted by gusts. I had recollections of paradise, the medals of boasts, and why not? I needed to recuperate and fast. Dan, the crapulous blighter, was pawing at my prone form.

'Get up, you miserable arse-candle ...'

I thought: Dan Albright is one of those good-looking fellows who don't realise that women dislike them. But I was wrong. Dan had always been a spotter of phonies, and he knew that I was. But a spotter of phonies generally recognises truth too, despite insincerity, and he knew that I did love Melania. What was there to prove? She bent her spondlespank ear to my mouth and I said: 'I love you, Mel.'

I was suddenly being mopped up and down by various people, none of whom I recognised. Skullcrush was less; earpang receding. Mel the wizardess was speaking ...

'Look, we're who we should be with. Me and him. You and Arlesie ... where is she? She should be here.'

'She's abseiling the facade!', 'She's shimmying down the drainpipe!', and 'She's going to die!' were what I heard as I got to my feet.

Out on the landing Josh was pedantically snogging Elloway who, I now noticed, was wearing a T-shirt that read YOUR FACE MAKES MY PUSSY DRY. Well, a doctor could cure that, surely. The very man; a perfect match. In an inspired and pregnant spirit I said:

'Aaww, blessèd be you and your kin.'

This was not the best thing to say in front of my cousin Daniel Albright (celebrity photographer — perhaps you've heard of him

87

— award-winning chef, kickboxing champion and *deeply religious person*).

'What is this foul ignorance?' he asked.

'Gosh, cuz, I do seem to be annoying you this evening. I never thanked you for coming.' Still mildly stunned from the assaults and the booze, I went on: 'but did I mention you are looking wonderful, ravishing, fulsome?'

'Huh?' gawped Dan. 'Are you going gay for me?'

'No,' said Arlesienne, 'that would be silly.'

We all looked round, but she wasn't there, alas. Things picked up after that. I discoursed to everyone about my clapperboard-themed hall, the fans hidden in the fireplace for correct smoke direction, and the bathroom glass that frosted at touch. My house was a glorious thing indeed, but now no more than second-best. Melania Hirsch was on my arm, making everything sweeter.

* * * *

'I do.'

'And do you, Melania Hirsch, take Ralph Albright to be your lawfully wedded husband?'

'Oh, yes, *yes*, I do!' There was a mild cheer. 'Let's go *do a daddy*,' she whispered.

And we all lived spunkily ever after.

One Angry Man

for C.V.W.

who knows why, or should

All the computers were bright red. The work surfaces were yellow, the walls were blue and the landlines were green. Altogether, the third floor. On the second floor the work surfaces were red, the phones were yellow, the walls were blue and the computers were green. On the first and ground floors the remaining permutations were expressed. This arrangement greatly irritated the people who had to work in the building; those people who flitted up and down from colour to colour. They interpreted the scheme as an insult to their ability to remember which floor they were on. In truth, the building was deliberately tailored so as to advertise the totality of its constituent schema. Software, hardware, communications, furniture and exterior fabric were the product of one complete contract — the apparent inconvenience of the colour-scheme only served to advertise the singularity of the organic control that could be imposed on a single office building, a vertical slice of working space.

Abigail knew this, because she was stuck on the ground floor, reading the brochure in the lift. She had time to read most of it while her clearance was being processed.

Cal was deliberately slowing her down. When the phone call from reception came through she'd been backing up personnel files for the fifth time that day. The loud *shring* delivered her from her reverie of mindless routine. She waited for the third *shring* to sound out before plucking the receiver: answer too quickly and it shows you're not doing anything, answer too slowly and you're too far from your desk.

'Alpha Subject Containment Services. How may I help you?'

'Spare it. It's Melania. Downstairs. Ground floor. We've got the Archbishop.'

'The Archbishop of Canterbury?'

'That's the one.'

'*Christ.*'

'Not yet. Just the Archbishop. She wants to feed the Angry. Or something. Apparently.'

'Christ.'

'*Right*. Reverend-bleeding-heart. Right here in the lobby. What do I do?'

Cal looked at the Angry. The Angry waved. She hated that. May be she'd spray him later on. Give him something to whimper about. His ceiling was festooned with a great many cylindrical nozzles and she had a great many buttons to play with.

'The Archbishop can wait in the lift,' she decided. Yes, she bloody well could.

* * * *

The lift hummed a selection of ambient classics to itself as it idled, then propelled the Archbishop to her rendezvous with the Angry. Barber's *Adagio For Strings* synthesised and reimagined with a surprisingly unobtrusive drum track, *Hey Jude*, and *The Girl From Ipanema* rendered as a tango, for some vague reason. Colours flashed by. Abigail started worrying, not for the first time that day, about her costume. Purple blouse, long black skirt, green jacket — too much like a uniform. The bands weren't working for her, she decided, ruefully. Back to the old dog collar on Monday. Horrible thing. She'd recently been attempting a looser collar that could have been described as a studied update of eighteenth century clerical bands. The resulting effect looked twee and Victorian. *Damnation!*

The first six months of Abigail Singer's incumbency had been, she supposed, absurdly dominated by media discussions of her wardrobe. She had therefore quickly applied herself to the problem of devising a clerical uniform for herself which provoked no comment of any kind. This proved the hardest sartorial invention of all and she had to admit that it was accordingly absorbing a disproportionate slice of her attention.

The doors *frished* open and Archbishop Abigail saw a big room full of freestanding computers, furnished with a single desk. At the far end of the room was a great cage, and inside the cage a perspex box. There were only two people in the room: a woman seated behind the desk who refused to look up or even acknowledge the lift's arrival, and a hairy man with his back to her, inside the box inside the cage.

The Archbishop did not hesitate, but strode over to the desk and introduced herself. She looked straight at Cal, and Cal looked straight past Abigail with eyes that betrayed weariness and measured contempt. Clever Abigail was indulgent, seeing someone warped by the occupation of denial, whose only professional power was to deter, to inhibit and delay. She blinked, looked again and tried to love, but her time was short. She needed to thwart this woman, and quickly.

'You're here to see the Angry?'

Archbishop Abigail nodded.

'He's over there. You can see him from here.'

Abigail didn't look. She sighed, 'I have to get in there. I have to talk to him.'

'Our insurance won't cover it.'

'I've dealt with all that. No one here has any liability. I signed all that away weeks ago.'

'Then I'd better show you this.'

Cal reached into her desk and produced a yellow folder stuffed with photos and printouts. Then she fanned them out. The photos were all recent and all hairy — simple and oft-produced sensationalist pictures of any anonymous Angry — nothing here that could be readily identified as Barny Poulcher — the Angry the Archbishop was here to see. Cal nodded and gathered them back. Then she reached for the other photos. These as-yet unpublished new photos were clearly of Barny Poulcher, the first recognised Angry, who had unwillingly become something of the poster child of the condition. Floodlit flesh discoloured by bruises, pocked and perforated by tiny cuts — veins of red crisis, purple lace, blown-up and exposed. Barny's eyes like those of a reptile, waiting, waiting.

'Multiple and compound bruising, severe abrasions and head injuries … All adding up to a violent record, wouldn't you say?' declared Cal triumphantly, as Abigail looked from print to print. Acknowledging the evidence with brows knotted in outrage and concern.

'But … But these are all self-inflicted injuries!'

'You seem disappointed.'

'It's a colossal injustice! He hasn't hurt anyone!'

Cal sat straighter and shuffled her papers like a newsreader. Mildly fidgety. Lunch was only an hour away and she intended to spend as little of that hour listening to pious tosh as possible. 'This man worked with children. For six years. He ran literacy classes. He drove minibuses. He took them to wildlife sanctuaries, to ice rinks ... *Swimming pools*. Parents are now suing, as you know. *I* wouldn't like to be the one who gave an Angry a job like that.'

'Karen Laconte, you mean? No, you wouldn't. You wouldn't like to be her at all. She's left the country. When the story on Barnaby Poulcher broke she had all her windows broken and her house was vandalised every day for a fortnight.'

'She let a psychopath look after people's kids every day for six years. I'd say she's gotten off lightly.'

Abigail stared into the same face of stubborn hostility she had had to contend with ever since she took up this cause. No Entrance — No Surrender. Implacable.

'There's a man locked up in a cage over there, and there's no record of his ever having harmed a fellow human being. Fact. How do you cope with that?' The Archbishop leaned over the desk and glared at Cal with all the righteous verve at her disposal. Cal stirred her coffee with a biro and replied mechanically without looking up:

'We could do it your way of course. We could wait till he slices up a few children. Then we cage him, and then you get the visitors asking how well you're coping. Shall we try it that way round?'

'Why do you hate him?'

Shocked by such a direct question fired at her by so distinguished a personage, Cal looked up, dropped the pen into her coffee and immediately spoke the truth. 'Because he keeps me here.'

'Take me to him.'

They walked, accidentally in step, toward the box at the end of the room, its hairy prisoner still standing with his back to them. From top to toe he/it seemed to Abigail to be quivering, although this could have been the refractive effect of the perspex. Outside the transparent cube, the outer layer of cornering, the steel cage, accentuated the dangerousness of the Angry. Cal and Abigail came to a halt. Indented and illuminated, the title on the box hung perilously in midair. The words seemed strange when spelt out in full:

Acquired Neurally Generated Response Irritation Syndrome Subject Alpha — 09/08/2014

Cal said: 'When the cage door opens walk through immediately. The door closes after three seconds. It could slice you in two and I couldn't do a thing about it.' She tapped in a twelve digit code.

The door opened and Abigail stepped forward. Then it clanged shut, leaving Cal behind. Abigail turned, momentarily peeved by this sudden, expected abandonment. Cal smiled and reached through the bars of the cage.

'Here's an entry card. It self-destructs on application. When you want to leave just pick up the phone. If he gets nasty just slam a panic button and I'll spray him. He hates that. He *cries*.'

* * * *

Ninety seconds later she stood opposite the Angry. He hovered awkwardly, trying to be polite. It was clear he was unable to remember how to smile sanely.

'Sir?'

There was only the plastic bed. It looked unprepossessing. The Angry sensed her hesitation and swept the sheet and duvet to the floor with an energetic swoop of the arm. He/it kicked the resulting debris under the bed and made a *please-be-seated* gesture. 'I should have cleaned up a bit. But I didn't get much notice. They won't let me hear the news. Any news. Thank you for agreeing to see me.'

The Archbishop sat down and waited for him to speak again.

'I'm sorry to be so hairy. I must look quite objectionable. But there is a regime here and sharp objects of any kind don't feature. I'll be strip-searched … and … you know … after you've gone, to see that I haven't swiped a lethal hair-clip, or a sharp comb or anything.'

'I didn't know that would happen. I should have thought.'

'That's all right, it's no big deal. Actually what happens is, I pin *myself* down so that they can come in. They spray me until I've handcuffed one wrist to the bed-frame — cuffs are built into the frame, as you can see — they snap-lock. I've tried arguing with them on this point. What *I* say is that all they have to do is *threaten* me with the spray and I'll handcuff myself. They do all seem to like playing with the spray though, and they especially like not giving me any warning. It's quite cold, but it would be okay if you could just brace yourself for it.'

'It's no sort of life for you here.'

'It is astonishing though, objectively speaking, all the technology that goes into keeping me humiliated. If I could stand back only a bit and see it from a distance, I think I'd be rather admiring.'

'You can do all that when you get out.'

Barny Poulcher bit his lip. A nozzle on the ceiling twitched. The conversation had just been ruined. 'Not something I think about. Can't happen. Won't happen.'

'*Must* happen.'

Barny winced and started pacing the box. He scratched the back of his neck in frustration. 'You won't fill any pews with that kind of crazy talk. You're onto a real loser here. I'm a very unsatisfactory victim. There are no votes to be had by being nice to Angries. We are popular anathema right now. You'll be making enemies simply by being here. I bet you've made quite a few already, now, haven't you?'

They came in to her home and cathedral by landline, mobile phone, email, snailmail, social media and much more, their illiteracy shaking with rage:

ANGRIES KILL CHILDREN YOU FUCKED UP BIATCH
I HOPE YOU DY SOON — YOU AND YOU'RE KILLA FRIEND
GOD WILL PUNISH YOU SLOWLY. I WILL KILL YOU
KWICKLY
HOPE YOU HAVE KIDS AND WATSCH THEM DIE YOU
MORRON

'I've had some negative feedback,' she admitted.

'They won't let me see any papers in here. They do all the thinking for me, I'll be bound.' A flaky smile accompanied the anachronism. 'I mustn't swear or they'll spray me. I mustn't become agitated. I must use only reasonable words. If I sound rather strange or if my diction becomes slow or stilted or there's an expletive that craves utterance ...' Barny paused and wiped his forehead. 'And I'm expensive, aren't I? People are resenting the amount of taxpayers' money I cost.'

Abigail dropped her head in shamefaced confirmation.

'People think this is the Ritz. They look at how expensive I am and assume I'm having a ball. It's the way people are brought up to think. They used the same trick on gypsies and hippies and Travellers in the old days. I remember reading up on it for my sociology course. They'd spot a convoy of vehicles crammed full of suitable undesirables, then they'd get the police to track them by helicopter. Then they'd go on TV citing the monumental helicopter bill and blame it on the Travellers. The Travellers end up being blamed for stealing taxpayers' money to pay for the helicopter. Then while everyone was getting stewed up about ... the whole business, they'd shut down a few coal mines, or do something else in a hurry ... or privatise something. That's why I'm here. I'm the culmination of the process. I'm the end-point.'

Abigail seized on this last remark. Barny's reflective sociology was saving her a lot of time. 'That's it! You see it clearly. *You* ... You can be the point where it all turns around. If you're vindicated, the whole scapegoat thing comes to an end.'

Barny took a step back and opened both eyes wide, shiny and spooky like those of the young Robert Powell. 'So that's why you're here,' he smiled, 'you want me to be your *christ* ...'

A shot of liquid leaped out at him and zapped both eyes. Barny screamed.

The Archbishop took off her scarf and wiped his eyes with it.

'Keep the scarf,' she suggested.

'I can't. I might strangle someone with it.' He returned the scarf and shook his head. The spray had been so precisely aimed that not a drop had touched Abigail. 'It's the silly computer. The familiar name for Messiah it treats only as an expletive. That was a warning shot. I get four or five a day, on average.'

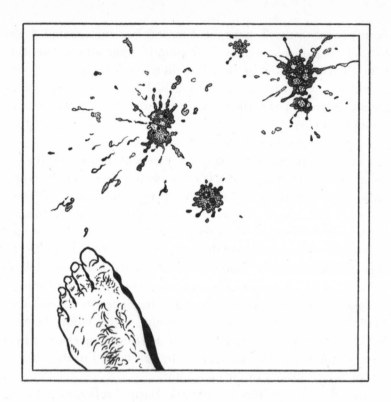

'Even I feel like swearing and I've only been in here five minutes.'

'Oh, you can eff and blind as much as you like — the computer only objects to me doing it.' He resumed pacing up and down. 'Anyway, Messiah … the Nazarene thing … no can do. Sorry. Won't work. I can suffer, sure, but can't triumph. And I can have no disciples.' He stopped and looked at her. 'And I can't heal anyone. And I'll die relatively soon and stay dead and loathed.'

'We can release you in the name of everyone's freedom.' She briefly wondered why these things sounded so naff, when coming from her mouth.

'I can't be free. Where can I move to? Who's going to welcome a chemically determined psychopath into a street full of children? A *whole world* of children?'

'You've never hurt children.'

'Yes, true, but I'm programmed to hurt children. All the tests say so. The courts say so. The mothers of these children say so.'

'I want to save children from the people who put you in here.'

'They won't listen to the likes of you or me. Even if you are Catholic.'

'Who knows? Who do you think they are — these people?'

The Angry stopped short of his full stride and swivelled round in recognition of what he regarded to be a good question. He put his hands behind his back and stared up to see if any of the nozzles were moving. Then he began to tell his story

'You know, I only went in for an injection. Tiny insect bite it was. They all said I should have it looked at. "Better safe than sorry." That was at the hospital, a year ago last December. Then I get a phone call from the hospital asking if I could come in for a full check-up, and X-rays. I'm worried, but I do just that. Next thing I know, I'm waking up to dogs, megaphones, police snipers, all the way down Pond Street. Five in the morning. The local Residents' Association was up in arms till they found out more about me. Since then I've been taken to various places. It was the bruises that got them frightened — see? The blood tests and the bruises together. I was very unlucky in that I happened to be bruised at the time.'

'Why do you bruise yourself?'

'Ah, well. I don't, as a rule. It's a rare thing, actually. It's been blown out of all proportion. It just so happened I'd bruised myself quite recently, which meant they were pouring over my samples with special vigour. They're still at it right now. My fluids are travelling all over the world as we speak. Odd feeling really. I've never left Europe, but now bits of me are visiting more than fifty countries simultaneously without me having to leave this box.'

'You must be freed. Unless you are freed then human beings have no moral reference points left. We cannot judge the ethics of any action while people can be excoriated on the basis of some sociopathic chemical predetermination.'

Barny felt like applauding this accurate succession of long melancholy words. But he restrained himself. She might want to visit again, and he couldn't pretend he didn't want that.

'Of course, you're in the Good and Evil market, aren't you, judging, dividing, condemning, rewarding? Tell me. How are you on abortion?'

'I'm against. By-and-large. In essence.'

'I'm Pro-Choice.' And he grinned, horribly, lips tight shut.

Dear God, thought Abigail, he's wishing he'd never been born. He's wishing he'd never existed so as to save all those people who are going to be bred-out because of him. Abigail realised that her time was short, and that the Angry had reached a point beyond the need for tact or timing.

'What's it like?' she asked, suddenly.

'When I become — *angry*?'

'When you become that.'

'*Heat*,' said the Angry, and momentarily felt it. 'Heat and blurred vision. Something happens to the digestive system, something churns away at you. Then there's a moment when you see yourself from the outside. You fly right out of your body and watch yourself along with other people acting or being frightened of you — the hot beast, shaking and sobbing inside the body. And then when the temperature is just right, I hit. Sometimes. Sometimes I only hit once. Sometimes I hit myself the second time because I've hit myself the first time. The second hit is in recognition of the extreme situation of hitting myself at all. Then I pile on the blows because I have to be confirmed within the extremity of my condition. I can't be partial anathema — I have to be total. Give me a bunch of grapes and I can't eat a few, I'll eat the whole bunch. I stress the fact that this sequence is a very rare occurrence.'

'Do you always hit yourself? Does it never go outwards?'

'Not so far. Physically. But it all happens in a nanosecond.'

'Has it ever happened in here?'

Barny twitched and started again to scratch the back of his neck. Immediately he spotted one of the nozzles on the ceiling swivel in his direction. He quickly put his hands in his pockets and recomposed his features.

'It happened once. It was part of an experiment they were doing. They dropped a selection of my weekly hate-mail through the ceiling. See, I … I was upset. And I let myself down rather badly. Let's talk about something else.'

So they talked about everything. The walls grew thin and the world came close. They held hands. Long hair blew away from Barny's wide face, and spaces of pink comic humanity emerged. A thirty-six-year-old man and a sixty-five-year-old woman alone together and animated in a big glass box.

'You're special. I love you,' said the Archbishop suddenly. 'God loves you. I'm here for *you*.'

Barny Poulcher climbed down onto his knees and looked up at her for what seemed like a full minute. He started to sway backwards and forwards, very gently. 'You mean that?' he said, straight at her.

'Ask me for something. *Anything* a human being can do, I'll do, or perish trying …'

'I know you will.'

'Ask me.'

'I'd love a razor.'

'That's all?'

'It's asking a huge amount. A safety razor and scissors. Or maybe just scissors.'

Then Abigail understood. 'They justify not giving you a razor by saying it's a weapon and then wait for you to become alarmingly hairy enough to be someone who looks like someone who ought to be kept away from sharp objects of any kind. Then they send photos to the press.'

'I think so, yes. They took a fresh batch just this morning.'

Abigail also fell onto one knee. Still taller than him, she stared at Barny's forehead, filling her field of vision. She pondered its lines and its colours. Its unique cartography of red deserts and cruel canyons — all the slow deformities of personhood. Most of all she saw the map of flesh throbbing and shaking to the quick pulse of naked unhappiness. She reached out and kissed his brow, briskly but without revulsion, and felt the salt of a single tear rise up and pause in the corner of her eye.

She stood up and buzzed her way out.

'Don't forget the razor.'

Archbishop Abigail clenched a Power of Freedom salute without looking back. Straight past Cal she marched, and on into the lift. Colours flashed by and the earth loomed. She mechanically raised her arm to wipe away the tear, but then pulled it back. *Show the tear*, she decided. Not flaunt, not hide, but permit.

* * * *

Abigail goes to church to pray. Melania goes to lunch. Cal goes to the bars of the cage outside the box and pulls faces, and the Angry goes to faraway places in his safe hairy head, where human hearts sing in unison and the blood runs free, where love was once important, and children were allowed to be.

Bluebeard

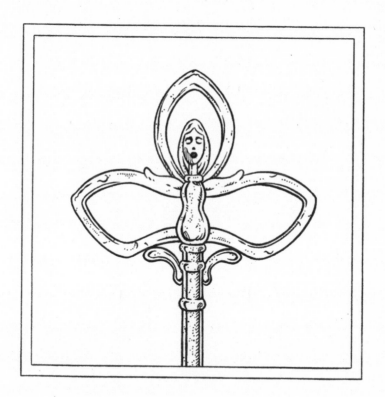

After the wedding ceremony — a modest affair with a standing buffet rather than a formal meal, and no guests on the groom's side, Bluebeard took his bride back to the house. *House* was a rather inadequate word, however, as she found when it heaved into view. Athalone was a dark place. Even the name was sombre, mournful. And it was enormous, with East and West wings and Cornetto minarets in the centre.

Bluebeard had lived there so long that no one in the town could recall if ownership was ancestral or he'd bought it. Either way, Bluebeard hadn't aged in many years. While not an obviously intimidating presence, the villagers avoided Bluebeard on his infrequent trips to town because of the mystery. We fear those who don't appear to need human contact. It seems we don't see them often. Many times he wore a stretched, quiet smile, which had the effect more than anything else of blindness. The private pleasure of his nature; personality lines drawn long.

His wife seemed an unusual choice: the gregarious daughter of a rich merchant named Hans Kansa, she had easy forsythia charm. Unused to suffering. Early twenties, teapot cheekbones, twice a winner of the town's little beauty contest. There was nothing materially boastful there — simple strength in biology. Her father was the wealthiest man in town other than Bluebeard himself, and strictly speaking, Athalone was three miles outside town.

From a droll point of view, it's easy to wonder at the attraction, but we shouldn't. Bluebeard, although old and publicly undramatic, had secure charisma that was undeniably attractive. For a girl who'd grown up with a powerful father it was a natural progression.

'So, finally, we are here,' said Bluebeard. 'My castle is not a place of celebration or gaiety, like your father's. Speak to me, are you coming?' He stepped down from the coach and extended his arm. Above Athalone's turrets, birds wheeled in currents.

'I'm coming darling Bluebeard. One moment, please.' She gathered her things and took his arm to step down onto the gravel. 'Are you coming?'

'Oh yes, darling Bluebeard.' The castle gates groaned open for them and she turned: 'I have left my family for you, darling Bluebeard, please never reject me. I love you wholeheartedly, darling Bluebeard, even as we cross your icy threshold.'

And they embraced before down three steps and on through the inner doors.

'Let the gates be closed and bolted fast behind us,' thundered Bluebeard. The hall they were in was vast and grey. Stairs to some crypt curved down from an arch to their right. On a high window-sill there was a smitheringale standing on one leg. She looked at it. Its head was rumpled, fern-like, soft to touch. It had never seen waves. She didn't reckon it was more than a few months old. Then it took off, a hint of dust. A beam of moonlight crossed the stone floor and began to move off into shadow, an animal craving some safe dark corner. 'Before I gaze at you again I'll need a time for tears. Before I gaze at you again, let hours turn to years.'

'Oh *darling* Bluebeard, love me.'

He took her blonde hand and led her deeper into Athalone. She noticed he had key-shaped irises, no cunning there, but much resignation in the face — oft-frowning, or perhaps merely restless. *He keeps the shadow of insignificance from my door*, she thought. The stupidity of impulsiveness.

'All who come here cease their gossip. All the rumours hushed in silence,' she said, holding him. Her head against his heart was where she longed to remain, inert. Blonde strands of her hair fanning out, electrified by love.

'My castle is too dramatic, perhaps. You are ordinary. But you possess a high value of warmth. Ignore the rumours of the village. Provincial ideas.'

'Oh darling *Blue*beard. My darling Blue*beard*.'

On they walked. Athalone loomed around them. It was an impressive place, yet bare, so unlike the bustling town. Teeming marketplaces, frenzied streets. Jugglers, hawkers, great magicians; Holy men smeared with ash, dead leaves and the souls of men.

'What is this moisture on the walls? The stones are sweating. My fingers weep to touch them. Why the shadow, *dar*ling Bluebeard? Everything is in shadow.'

'Ordinary, beautiful girl, I apologise. Wouldn't it be nicer in your father's house? Roses on the terrace, moonlight dancing?'

'*Never*, sweetest Bluebeard. I no longer care for sunlight or dancing. Roses are nothing to me now. I embrace solemnity.'

Athalone, to her, was a desertion of family, but not necessarily unhappy. She saw hope within its walls, and hope is a good thing.

'Perhaps the best thing,' said Bluebeard, 'is that you noticed. You have a deep vein of care. It shows sometimes, in your forehead.'

'Oh dar*ling* Bluebeard, with my warm arms I shall heat this place …'

'Athalone.'

'Yes, in Athalone I shall warm the cold marble, warm it with my body, let me do it, let me do it, let me!' she cried. And Bluebeard took her in his arms and sniffed her unusually blonde hair, which smelled of blueberries.

They dined together that night. The menu featured shellfish and lobster — the shelled family. Crusty. The table was long but Bluebeard sat next to his wife, and all was fine and good. Side plates teemed. He didn't need to dominate — didn't want to. A huge portrait of him hung at one end of the hall. It was enough. Athalone was no longer lonely. Bluebeard momentarily imagined a book wherein he was depicted emerging from a lake, old moobs dripping, creaky legs a-gangle.

'I shall fill your house with light,' she said. 'Glitterballs! Glitter on the fingers, glitter on the toes, let me love you, *darling Bluebeard*.'

He flinched. This was not unexpected. He had always attracted fleshy girls. This wasn't to do with care — although flesh can prove motherhood, Bluebeard had always married for love. Is this a good quality? Bluebeard was not at heart a bad man. But how to judge, with nothing to compare? She had had nothing, and now everything: but at what price? The impulses were right, in the body. They don't lie. Walls pressed in.

'No light may enter here. Nothing glitters in my castle.'

'It doesn't matter, *sweetest* Bluebeard, my darling, show me all over Athalone.'

Leaving the table, he took her arm. They walked on. Long shafts streaming from the topmost windows lost their light in dust motes on the way down and flickered at their feet like moths. She noticed that Bluebeard was skinny. It is not skinny people who look hungry, but rather the fat ones, she realised. However, despite their recent meal, Bluebeard looked famished. She noticed also that he lingered on the shortest words and sniffed at the end of every sentence. Perhaps this was connected to his thin frame, she didn't know. Unto himself, Bluebeard was a roaring centre. To her he was anything but. He was a surly beetle, propelling itself through sparse acres, legs akimbo, tongue dangling. And yet not: Bluebeard upstanding.

'There are five doors here, all bolted, locked from me. Why, darling Bluebeard? *My* darling Bluebeard?'

'No one must see what is behind them. Please, ask me not to open even one. I have so much forgetting to do before I try to gaze again on you.'

'Wind shall scour the rooms, light embolden them! Let the doors be thrown open for me, your wife, darling Bluebeard. Air will fill Athalone, happy sunshine will cheer on laughing breezes. Open them, open them all! For me, my darling! For me! Throw them open!'

Bluebeard held her close. He didn't yield. To him she seemed inconsequentially yielding. Some bake-faced girl, a bride, the supreme dullard's pin-up: lifeless to touch, inactive. His walls wept, sure, but Bluebeard wanted to please the bride. Her cheeks were tired. He parried. She turned and pulled him toward a door.

'Castle of sighing, castle of weeping, castle of glittering,' she said.

'No, alas, you underestimate me. Athalone is much, much more.' He dipped his head. They went on. The walls had a hundred eyes. Citadel of flesh. You can walk from place to place. You can pretend. If you can't place the rub, it's there: least expected. Here, there. And breathing out, breathing in — a choice all by itself. Huge corridors. Hope is a good thing, perhaps the best of things, but one can't guess at it. One hopes to, but stalls.

'*Oh* darling, my darling Bluebeard. I heard your castle give a sigh of anguish. My heart, my darling, come and let us open this door together. Both of us. I'll unlock it, only me — I'll do it gently, softly and gently. Nothing will hurt. Give me the key, *my* Bluebeard, because I love you so.'

Sadly, Bluebeard lowered. Sometimes he knew absolutes, appealing condensed outlooks. Eliminate the superfluous. The door swung open.

'This is not a room, it's a vagina,' she said.

The room was draped in vermillion. A bloody rectangle of a window on the far wall, fiery beams crossing the floor between them.

'Well? What do you see?' asked Bluebeard, his voice sounding deeper than before. 'Was it worth it?'

She was dismayed. Athalone sighed again, breath pouring back and forth. 'Oh sweet Bluebeard, there are shackles and daggers, racks, pincers and branding irons. This is your torture chamber, dearest Bluebeard. It frightens me so. It's horrible, horrible!'

'You are frightened, woman?'

'I love you, exal*t*ed Bluebeard. Your castle walls are blood-stained. The stone is bleeding, but I am afraid no longer. See, dawn is breaking, my frantic love.'

Bluebeard turned. Indeed, light was curling in. The high small windows had begun to glow. Dwelling smitheringales gone.

Suddenly she thought of her father and family: the rich merchant giving away his only daughter for a handful of promises; her mother dabbing her eyes and turning to the wall. She continued: 'Every door must now open! Give me the keys to all the others. We must enter through all these doorways because *I* love you, darling Bluebeard.'

'Through and through Athalone trembles. You may open the others. Stay away until you cross my mind barely once a day, stay away until I wake and find that I can say ...'

She interrupted. 'I shall be gentle and soft, my darling. Have hope, let it into your castle. It is a good thing.'

The door opened with a weak yellow glow. Beams of light from this door joined the red ones from the first. A flag was forming, marker of Athalone.

'What do you see?' asked Bluebeard, new notes sounding in his voice, a roguish indifference, a peculiar growling.

'There are piles of crowns, the spoils of war, oh cruel darling Bluebeard, countless fearful weapons of battle, arms and armour, *grande amore*. You are strong and mighty, my Bluebeard, but cruel, cruel.'

'... That I shall gaze at you again without a blush or qualm. My eyes will shine as new again, my manner poised and calm. Are you frightened?'

'Blood on all the spears and daggers. Your battle weapons are stained with the blood of other men. But I am not frightened. Give me the keys to the other rooms, they must be opened for me, your wife, light of everything, *my Bluebeard*. Open them for me because I love *you*.'

'I must warn you,' replied Bluebeard, 'Athalone's stones thrill with rapture. The blood that oozes is fresh and soothing and cool.'

'I came here because I *love* you, darling Bluebeard, my darling Bluebeard. Let us open every doorway! I love you and *adore* you!'

Bluebeard, with reviving grace and a certain crepuscular rankness, said: 'I warn you again, woman, wife, that you will not enjoy what you find behind these doors. I shall give you the final three keys, but know that you will lose me if you look therein.'

'Oh *silly* darling Bluebeard! My *most tender* Bluebeard. Let your castle be opened to the light. Let me help you, let me feel your feelings, let me live through you, my husband Bluebeard, let me feel. I do this for love.'

'I give you three heavy keys. But ask me nothing. Ask no questions, my wife, and you will be happy.'

She snatched the keys from his hand — outstretched, right. A hectic colour came into her eyes, the impulsiveness of propaganda. Pretty as a moth she was, fluttering *hoooooooeeeee*. Up above, sequins of lights came on, the beams moving into position. Narrow, with fish-like jaws, the beams advanced and receded, breathing. Natural posturing. What was her name? She no longer cared.

The door swung outward. Suddenly great vistas opened, Elobian chests stuffed with scrolls, Chinese mountains of gold. An orange beam joined the others, advancing.

'But this is beautiful, beautiful,' she said, 'such gems and jewels, gleaming rudderless rubies, gowns of ermine, pearls that beget queens, glinting coins, reflecting diamonds. More crowns, but this time of glory. Why do I feel alone?'

'Because you are nearing the time when you will understand what it is to be truly alone. This is my treasury. Enjoy it while you have time. Every crown shall be yours. Every ruby, pearl and diamond. All yours.'

'But ...' she said, '... all your precious finds are bloodstained ...'

This was true, but only to her eyes. Bluebeard saw things differently. A flake of a life was better than none. He loved deeply, but felt too much betrayed. She had promised to never betray him, and this may have been true, but she had already done it, without recognising so. She opened the next door.

A blue-green beam of light joined the others.

'What is this room?' she asked.

'It is the meeting point between who I am and who you are,' he replied. 'Do not go any further. Please, although this room is filled with beautiful flowers, all growing wonderful, with love like August sun, please do not ask to go any further. Your father would surely forbid it. He is a powerful man. You should not want to risk *his* wrath. So why mine? Athalone is sad already, without extra impetus.'

'What beautiful shrubs, what fragrant flowers; silky blue lilies tall as you, your castle's secret garden. Under rocks and boulders, lovely dazzling flowers!' she exclaimed.

Patterned in the sky, meteors soared, treadgold. People would purple under this sunset, children would skip carefree along the sand, tapping the tread. Faint lights dimmed to tiny seams with the first rain of the season. Bluebeard's mind was turning. While not an excitable man (it had something to do with leanness — he had eaten badly in the early years), he could be aggressive. There was a pesky upturn to the upper-lip. And yet he loved his wife and did not want her to suffer for his sake. He said: 'Are you afraid?'

'It only takes a thought to make me realise I love you, and your *sweet* fragrant garden, hidden under rocks and boulders.'

'This is indeed Athalone's secret garden. Your secret garden.'

'Ah, what tender flowers, giant chrysanthemums quiet as the souls of men, exquisite silky roses, red blossoms frothing with light

— never have I seen such beauty before.'

'Every flower nods to greet you, my wife. You make them bud. But just as fast they wither before you, knowing what you …'

'Oh dar*ling* Bluebeard, the white rose is flushed with bloods-pots. The soil is bubbling, blood-soaked …'

'It is your eyes that open the buds. Praising you they sing of dawn …'

'Oh Bluebeard, my darling sweetest *husband*, who has bled and died to feed your secret garden?'

Athalone has a character. Is it female or male or other? We don't care. Athalone picks up or drops people as it sees fit. We come and go, breathing in and out. Like victims of some airborne illness (the chief symptom of which is prolonged slumber), we vacillate. Thick, blue and pulsing (and always carping disgruntlements), we remain. But waiting for what recognition?

We go on; you stop. Who cares? The world keeps turning despite you, whether by accident (your invisible inconsequentiality) or design (you're hated everywhere). The world can touch your fingers and the world can touch your cheeks. The world can do things we cannot because we are useless, eager yet boring, hopeful yet shallow. Athalone will root you out anyway. Lateral emotions rise here, in this light-changing schism.

'Ask no questions, dear wife, if you love me. Look — Athalone gleams and brightens. My fifth door is beckoning.'

'Thank you my darling Bluebeard, *dearest* darling Bluebeard.'

'Stay far away my love, till I forget I gazed at you today. So blonde, so fair and admirable.' And as he slid the key into the lock, he added, 'please go no further.'

Was this some sexual idea, an erotic impulse writ large? Blue-beard had never considered the possibility; she *had* considered it. For her this was something paramount. Her father had demanded to know if, and if so why, his daughter had decided to love a man with a reputation.

Can you *decide* to love someone? It does happen — lavish feelings in play. Bluebeard had decided, definitively, but with a few smallish rules. It's hard, no one would deny. To him the 'Good Wife Rules' were simple: Don't go away. Be by my side.

His was not a battle-of-the-sexes — it was a repudiation of his childhood, a childhood that had included infringements on the states of childhood. Bluebeard didn't see women in the way usual men saw women. He saw them in a religious way, a male way, of course. Faith justified this, but also poisoned all that was moral. Seen this way, Bluebeard was the common one — it really was so. He was a godly paragon. But he wasn't ordering her to cover her face and hair, or have her sexual organs sewn up or sliced off, although he could have done, being the particular lord of this domain.

And what reputation? The whole town knew that Bluebeard had married several times before. No one knew how many times: do *you* know? Some had been present at this wedding or that one. Some claimed to remember some of the wives' names — Elloway, Pikaia, Arlesienne — although these rumours were unsubstantiated. What gossip remained however, concerned their disappearances. Bluebeard had never been observed to divorce, but neither had a wife been observed to leave Athalone. Reputation is nothing, of course. It is merely a moan or praise that means nothing to anyone, really, save the gossiper. Gossip is addictive and aimless, non-rhetorical. Reputation is what they say about you, and if you're even slightly clever, it won't matter a jot. Then again, wandering down corridors doesn't auger well for self-improvement. It's no fluke that the most politically important places in the world are precisely designed to solve the problem of such wanderings.

Today, thought Bluebeard, I lost my love to geography. Stone walls took my bride. She asked too much and too soon. I loved her though — and let that past tense be heard around these same walls. This will be the final time a woman does this to me. They are blood-keepers, keepers of the blood; and timekeepers, keepers of the time. I let her through and she follows the path. As a man, he thought: *who cares about doors and keys if you already have my heart?*

'Let the fifth door be flung open,' he shouted, suddenly. Resolved at last.

Music dazzled the hall, cascading from the opening. Huge sounds, vibrating organ, full pipes, strings a-frenzy, brass ablaze.

Shielding her eyes from a violent indigo ray was for her the gesture of a moment.

'Look, woman: now behold my splendid kingdom, the spacious vistas, sand-blown savannahs. Is it not a noble, sensible place?'

There was silence. She stared, pupils fixed on invisible webs.

'Fair and spacious is your country,' she whispered.

'Silken meadows, velvet forests, tranquil streams of winding silver, lofty mountains, purpling and hazy.'

'Fair and spacious is your country.'

'All is yours, my dearest wife, for ever. Here both dawn and twilight flourish, here sun, moon and stars dwell — your undying playmates they will be.'

'Fair and spacious is your country. But darling Bluebeard, my darling Bluebeard, why are the clouds bloodstained? Why does blood seep from every leaf?'

Athalone is male, I think, despite the blood. Its blood is of treachery, dishonour, not of the female kind — the life-giving, or of the other — noble and blind. *Hoooooooeeeee* sing the thankgoodness birds in the red trees, plied with purple fruit. Barrowloads of truffles should be found there, also weeds galore, the usual. The undertow pulls in and releases nothing. Be careful of the undertow. I never had a reason to live so long. But then I never needed a father. What lies.

Bluebeard wasn't a father. Not cut out for it. He was tall, leaning, with tiny, pushed features. A Disney nose — exaggerated curve — cheeks cliff-white, forehead-led. Inspiration creased in the delicate expensive neck, an afterthought of some random god. Benevolent or otherwise, Bluebeard was going to get it. 'My castle now glitters, as you said it would, always said it would. Your hands have done this, darling wife. Your hands are blessed. Place them on my glitterball heart.'

'There are still two doors left to open, darling Bluebeard, *my darling Bluebeard.*'

'Alas, those two must stay unopened. Now shall Athalone ring with music, now shall all the shadows vanish before you ... Come, my love. I yearn for you to kiss me.'

'Let the last two doors be opened ...'

'Are you coming? I await your kiss. Come, and love me, your husband.'

'Let the last two doors be opened first ...'

Love is a sickness, thought Bluebeard, a surrendering of sanity, and for what? Does it justify children? Or will the children come — how we long for those fresh faces — despite love? Surely consonantal contentedness accounts for them. Hope in love sketches a torso in the air, whose we do not know. The smile suggests plumpness — health. The white and blue of unreluctant, smiling eyes.

'Child, I warn you. You wanted sunlight. It is here.'

She almost screamed: 'Two more remain. Not one of these great doors must remain fast against me. I love and adore you, darling Bluebeard, do it for our love. Even if I perish for us, I shall fear nothing, dearest Bluebeard. Open them, open them all, *mighty* Bluebeard! Open them!' His wife held out her hand. Not demanding, now merely expecting.

'Come, I shall give you one more key.'

Athalone gave a deep sob as it turned.

'Are you afraid? What do you see? Was this worth it?'

'I see a sheet of water, pale-green and trembling. Tranquil, sleeping it is. Breathing. But what is this water?'

The lake spread before them gave the silent impression of being on the very edge of the world. Odourless and subzero, a place of emptiness and scuttling dangers. Utterly flat.

'It is tears, my darling, tears. Not the tears of those whom I have vanquished in battle or even of those whom I have crushed beneath my kingly feet. They are *your* tears, my love, your tears that will come. Before I gaze at you again I'll need a time for tears ...'

'Hushed, sleeping, glinting green, unearthly smooth ... yet ...'

'... Before I gaze at you again let hours turn to years. Come, woman, let me kiss you, I am waiting. The last door *must* remain closed. I am your husband — this is our wedding morning — come and kiss me.'

Out of this rough stone, we forge existence. Those who live by instinct are at the mercy of those who don't. Loving uselessly is worse than misreading love. Or more painful — it stops short of the final. Show us the mettle of your past time. Bluebeard considered it his right to take his wife in his arms, but it was not. How can one have rights over another? Perhaps we should seek clarity: How can one have rights over another without the backing of belief?

Yet she continued to surprise. She said, 'Do you really love *me*, Bluebeard? Truly, deeply?'

'You are and have always been my castle's daylight. Kiss me. Ask no questions.' His skin was leathery in the beam of green light that joined the others across the stones.

After a beat of an embrace, she said: 'Darling Bluebeard, tell me, tell me who you loved before me.'

'Ask me nothing. Not this. No more questions. I ask only for your future. I care nothing for your past. Kiss me, my bride.'

'But in what way did you love her? Was she fair? Did you love her more than me, *darling* Bluebeard?'

'Love me. Ask no questions.'

'Tell me truly, *mighty* Bluebeard.'

She was hungry now, he could sense. An unpleasant sensation. Two robots kissing each other, tin heads knocking, a rose clasped in a pincer, metal arms feeling for a heartbeat — that which keeps us human — and finding nothing. But still the rose is offered. Robots cannot be hungry, except for information. His wife would consume every scrap, every throwaway titbit of his past and hurl it out, in anger perhaps, or most likely insecurity. Bluebeard considered the proposition before dismissing it. He replied:

'It is true that you are not my first, but I love you and thus for me you are my first. My previous marriages, and I cannot change the past no matter how much regret attains, did not mean as much to me as you do. We must proceed by trust, and we must respect love.' In truth, he felt like a tin robot. He had no problem with loving her. The problem lay with her inquisitiveness, the natural (or at least indulged) female progression. Perhaps he was a misogynist. Since Bluebeard had loved all his wives wholeheartedly, this didn't seem credible, and yet ... And yet ... 'Then open the seventh and last door, if you must,' he said. 'I beg you not to, but fear that this sentiment will not aid your decision. I have so much forgetting to do before I try to gaze again at you.'

117

'I have guessed your secret, dearest husband. I *know* what you hide.'

If you know, he thought, *why persist? And, perhaps more importantly, why did you marry me? It seems to matter to* me. *I married in good faith — that should have been properly discussed before I gave you my heart.* He didn't retort, however.

She continued: 'Bloodstains on your warriors' weapons, blood upon your crown of glory, the blood-boiling soil of your garden, blood-streaked clouds in your sky. Now I see it all, Bluebeard, you cannot fool me anymore, Bluebeard, I know whose weeping filled your mineral lake …'

'Yes, as I said …'

'… All your former wives have suffered as I suffer …'

'How on earth do *you* suffer? I've given you what you wanted. And dinner was fantastic, I thought …'

'… the brutal bloody murders they told us of in the town. The rumours — truthful rumours, I'll prove every detail. Give me the last key. Open the last of your doorways!'

He opened his palm. As the last door opened, its violet beam joined the others in a rainbow across the cobbles.

'This is the room of hearts. The hearts I have loved and cherished. Here are my former loves.'

The air began to move, to rise towards them.

'*What?* They are *alive?* They live and breathe?'

'With radiant, royal, almost matchless beauty, indeed they live. They are the Immortals.'

'What do you mean?'

'*See.*' Bluebeard gestured into the seventh room. 'They have gathered all my riches, they have bled to feed my flowers. They have enlarged my kingdom. All my treasures are now theirs.'

One by one the former wives came forth with proud steps. Bodies ablaze with priceless gems, each wore a crown, but their expressions were blank and cold. Bluebeard sank to his knees in front of them and raised his arms heavenward. Not reaching out, but forward.

Humans are hot-wired to doubt the passionate and believe the vulgar, the easy, the holy. Yet, at the end, love is what there is, and

Bluebeard had clearly loved. Loved with sadness or with too much reliance; loved with fury and not enough thought. He had believed once too, as most have, but found only decrepitude. Why do we adore, when one of its opposites, disappointment, is so clearly the case? Adoring has many other opposites of course — reason and morality without justification among others. True adorers can't countenance any opposites. That's a crucial part of adoring. It may be that we have to go that route, but let's hope not. And hope is a good thing, perhaps the best of things.

Elloway, Pikaia and Arlesienne stood in a line and beckoned for Bluebeard's fourth wife to join them.

'Such speechless beauty,' she murmured, 'beauty beyond believing. Compared with these, I am nothing.'

Elloway's crown had tartan strips between carved African fauna in silver. Pikaia's, bald eagles straddling a gold snake design, and Arlesienne's faded in and out of focus, like breathing. Was it there or merely an illusion? It flickered as twilight. They were all striking people — queens every one. Their lands missed them, but Bluebeard had conquered, and not through striking. He got to his feet and said: 'Elloway, my first wife, I found at daybreak, crimson early morning — she is now the swelling sunrise with its cool mantle, she is its gleaming crown of silver, she is the dawn of every new day.'

'She is far richer and more deserving than I am. I am sorry, I am frightened, darling Bluebeard, my darling Bluebeard, please do not go on. She is enough.'

'Pikaia, my second wife, I found at noon. Silent, flaming, golden-haired noon. She is every noon hereafter, the heavy burning mantle, the crown of glory. She is the blaze of every midday.'

'She is far fairer than I,' said wife number four, joining the line. 'Please stop, *oh darling Bluebeard.*'

'My third wife, Arlesienne — oh, *French* girls. My travels in Europe took me through many places and I met many girls. Arlesienne stood me up for our first date. She should have been there, but was not. Still, I loved her, and didn't mind. Sometimes one must accept such treatment, in deference to the girl's self-esteem. She covets, yet won't admit.'

The world can touch your fingers and the world can touch your toes. *The world can do things I can't*, she thought, as she waited in line. There was nothing for her to say. She couldn't even remember her own name.

'Arlesienne I found at evening, quiet, languid, sombre twilight. She has the returning sunset. All that belongs to her. She flickers in my vision, the solemn sundown, the crown of ...'

'No more, *my* Bluebeard, please no more. I am still here. Please be my darling, oh Bluebeard.'

Why is it so? We cannot all be philosophers. Bluebeard found himself thinking across his life, down the corridors of it, into the turns and runs, the runts and urns. What *was* there, after all? And what was *there*? A wonderful way to win friends? Not at all. Humans are complicated, but it didn't have to be that way, so ferry me down. Friends come and go, they shuffle through, but people believe and will always adore. A distinct paucity of common sense. All the doors are now open. Every one. No bomb that ever burst shatters the crystal spirit. The women enter. Yes, yes, and yes. But then ...

'The fourth I found at midnight. Starry, ebony-mantled midnight ...'

'Please, no more!' she cried, 'no more! I am still here, *sweet*est Bluebeard. I am here only for you.'

'Your pale face was a-glimmer, and splendid was your seaweed hair. Every night is yours hereafter, Linaia. All darkness yours to warm.'

'No, no, no, no, *no*,' Linaia pleaded, 'please, all-powerful Bluebeard.'

He thought her common, but Bluebeard was common too. Desperately ordinary in the sense of his heart — a natural and unfortunate fault, or trait, of most men. He was extraordinary in other ways, by all means, but his heart was inarguably common. However, he thought her common in other senses, and he may have been correct in this. The shadow of significance had come forth from a dark corner ... So, he was not lying when he said, 'You are truly lovely, passing lovely, the queen of all my brides, my best and fairest. Stand with me.'

Small sobs broke from Linaia's body, and she beat her hips with the sides of her fists.

'*No*, no, no, no …'

Bluebeard turned and walked back to the third door they had opened. His sallow, historical cheeks bathed orange. Moths fluttered *hoooooooeeeeee* in and around the beam. He went through the door. Elloway, Pikaia and Arlesienne dipped their heads, as if in supplication, or fear of punishment — the same thing, really. Linaia's eyes grew more fearful as her husband reemerged with a dark crown, crusted with flickering jewels, and a luxurious deep-veined cape.

'No, no, no *no* …'

Athalone reposed: this was what it wanted. The male character required it.

Linaia bowed her head as Bluebeard approached. She drooped — the jewels were heavy, such a burden to wear. He wrapped the cape around her. Cocooned.

'Henceforth all shall be darkness,' he said, as Linaia sank to her threadbare knees. 'As it was before …' he placed the crown on her head — she walked into the fused beam of light, fracturing a rainbow into myriad shapes and shades, 'and ever shall remain.' His skin was no longer leathery but simply worn, torn in places, pocked and dragged. Meaning was all. His speech slowed, as it always did, toward the end of a sentence. He sniffed at the short words, the the, the and, the was. 'All shall be midnight now,' he said, 'and you were my Actual, my perfect template, my grand love. *Senza rancore*, my Linaia.'

But she was already following Elloway, Pikaia and Arlesienne into the seventh room, wearing her crown, the many heavy jewels and the fabulous sorrowful cloak. Yes, yes, yes, and finally yes. Who's a philosopher? Who are these women? What is left?

Bluebeard raised his gaze. Tormented by a billion scattered embers, ever cut by the razor edges of their frozen prison, his eyes were bare. He was no longer a roaring centre, or even skinny. Like a magnified image, his torso puffed, bloaty.

He didn't like looking at bones. Why *would* you like looking at bones?

Athalone, he felt, was overstepping. Less a companion and support, now more an overbearing father. Bluebeard, non-conformist. But then: *where would I be without you? Athalone, my soul.*

Life was never like this. He stood up, slowly, the camera's plum. She would never know how fine she looked to him then. She was his Actual, the one he'd wanted through all the longish lonely years. Who knew, really, how long it had been? Do you, dear reader, know? Perhaps it was a hundred years ... But then perhaps merely seven.

Rivulets of tears came down his face. You feel for him? Do you, dear reader? Under dead clouds, beams from the high small windows shrivelled in dust. No light pertains — all is dark corners. Bluebeard cringed. He knew he could change tense.

* * * *

It's odd to be a man. Life can be beautiful, but not in the way men want it to be, funnily. That *funnily* should be *oddly*, but then the paragraph would have to begin ... It's funny to be a man, but not in the way men want it to be, oddly. Same difference. Breathing out, breathing in, some kind of choice all by itself. Until it stops. Men can't *feel life.* They are not timekeepers, keepers of the time. Bluebeard never bled to establish a hold on life. Men take that for granted, oh yes, they do, dear reader, they strain for the perfect. The Actual. But we're left with the rest, what time throws us, the children of time. *And what to do with the children?* Bluebeard thought. Thank god there are no children here.

Manners are the basis of society. Softly smouldering, we think we know better. But we never do, really, do we? Do *you* know?

Now nothing was of any use to him, Bluebeard turned and walked forth into the light, as the red, yellow, orange, blue, indigo, green and violet beams of the flag faded to nothing. At least there weren't any children. Would there be another wife, or another like Linaia?

Unlikely. But then we do adore.

You adore for me, Bluebeard, who loved too much and yet did so little. You imagine the lurid questions: What has the masculine got to do with Athalone? and Why, and how, do the former wives live? and Look what could have happened and did not.

Goodnight dear reader, and I hope this tale told a story of love and of hope. Remember, love's the last thing to go. Love is what remains, even after hearing, supposedly the last sense to leave. Yes, love's the last to go. You would simply turn to those you loved and say: 'I love you.' Ferry me down. And only then disappear into darkness.

I, Bluebeard, burst with love for Linaia, And for Elloway, Pikaia and Arlesienne. And for you, dearest, sweetest reader: I burst with love for you.

And you didn't even know her name until I told you.

* * * *

Heh, heh, heh, heh.

Heh, *heh*, heh, heh.

Heh, heh, *heh*, heh.

Heh, heh, heh, *heh*.

* * * *

You thought I'd gone, didn't you?
Now, *didn't you?*

Fellrain's Golem

Professor Max Fellrain boarded the train at St Gallen. The box in Luggage had been loaded in Zurich. With the German border still some way off, he quickly telephoned ahead to check the museum's arrangements, and then settled down to savour the last hours he had before his life changed.

Hey, what. He was feeling cheerfully philistine as he ordered the lobster. This was the find that would make his name! The attractively bleached waiter-ess-other had irritated. He felt expected to enjoy himself, and found this stressful.

Dark-eyed bungalows filled the windows while the Professor waited for his drink, red stone and banging plumbing. He could sense. The ice by the tracks was melting, atmosphere flavourless. In fields, dusty children quickly danced. How odd that they should. They reminded him of midges attacking the insides of a fluorescent light fixture.

'Sir, would you like lemon with that?'

The Professor waved his arm, vaguely. The waiter-ess-other wondered if he/she/they was/were addressing a genius or a fuck-wit. He had the aura of genius — sexually cunning eyes, typically obstructive cheekbones, shapeless hair. He didn't give a damn. Yet he/she/they sensed an atavistic streak — an old tortoise soaking up the last rays before bedtime, or death.

'Thank you,' he said, and began sipping delicately. In *Ordered South*, Robert Louis Stevenson wrote:

Herein, I think, is the chief attraction of railway travel. The speed is so easy, and the train disturbs so little the scenes through which it takes us, that our hearts become full of the placidity and stillness of the country; and while the body is being borne forward in the flying chain of carriages, the thoughts alight, as the humour moves them, at unfrequented stations …

In Luggage was a figure cast from mud and other organic material: leaves, animal waste, long-dead twigs and the souls of men. It was seven-foot-two long — high? — and Professor Max

Fellrain had been searching for it for most of his adult life. More precisely, he had been working for many years to prove its mere existence, when some clandestine scholarship had suggested an actual location. *Elusive as Columbo's wife* was a phrase much bandied about his department, referencing the TV detective played by Peter Falk, whose wife is often mentioned but never appears onscreen. Just one more thing. When he felt it within his grasp, albeit many shores distant, his heart didn't rejoice. That was too far to imagine, never mind hope. But hope is a good thing, and he realised he had long possessed it, a quality he thought dead, or at least impure, fake.

He sipped his drink and let his mind wander, rudderless. Frosty petals boomeranged about the train. *Relax.* This one was on him. Screw them all. Fellrain had always felt patience to be a form of loyalty, and so it was. It had paid out. And when he'd finally revealed the golem, in a disguised box in an attic in Paris, France, under rafters festooned with oily ravens, clucking and shuffling about, he'd felt nothing like celebration. Just observance of what was rightfully his.

Tranquillising rain beat the roof as dusk fell. Professor Fellrain finished his drink, sighed, and pulled his briefcase from the overhead metal rack. It was one of those Parisian ones, mock-aged and masquerading as a satchel, complete with cosmetic buckle. He took out a cloth and wiped his careful oval lenses in their faux-antique frames.

The years of searching had hardened him into what he was — not an easy or pleasant man, he'd be the first to say. He hated the word *pleasant*. Stuck in the throat. Unmarried, childless, parentless. Nomadic by nature, he felt untied to his two dusty offices, one at the university, the other at the Museum of Natural Sciences. There were many shades of cruelty in his smile. He could hardly wait to enjoy the reaction of the dismay-able multitudes to his golem. *His* golem. And Professor Max Fellrain did, by now, in a bold and assaultive manner, consider the golem his. Bring on the fight for it.

They entered a long tunnel and the sharp overhead light crested on his dishevelled curls. He felt air corkscrewing around him. As a young man of nineteen he had misbehaved, attending Dance

Clubs, and affectedly smoking a pipe. He still sometimes found himself thinking fondly of that stringy pipe-tobacco, moistly dark. Then one evening, at a burlesque show named *Three Socks In The Hallway* — Europe was like that then — he'd met a sweet girl, or so he thought. She was all Jerusalem colours, and her skin smelled of apples. He told himself he didn't know she was a whore, which absolved him of blame when he was diagnosed with gonorrhoea. More conveniently, it rendered her solely culpable. Shortly after this salutary experience, he crystallised into faith. The Godless figure of his youth could not be detected today. Frowns were a preferred method of communication. God had brought him his golem.

Respect from his peers would become more. *Fame* was required.

The train emerged from the tunnel into an early evening sky full of tiny candles. It was 9.18, December 23rd. A different waiter-ess-other came by, this one dark, like a Jew. Although a Jew himself, Max distrusted them, and this waiter-ess-other had just reminded him of Ada the Whore. *She*, who he blamed for the stain on his trust, for polluting the shiny waters and tearing down the Saturday-stunned portico of his childhood. Trees used to burst with bird-code. It was a front he put on then, he thought. The young, the helpless: the greatest liars.

He ordered a basket of sliced bread and a pot each of raita and hummus to dip it in. Cursed by a cervine sense of smell — to him all humanity stank — the raita induced mild nausea and he pushed it away.

* * * *

After the German border stop, where he urinated and made another telephone call to the museum, to re-check their arrangements, he briefly dozed, clutching his briefcase to his belly. But worry about the smell of his urine soon roused him — it had been sour, disillusioned. Much given to superstitions, Max felt that this was a bad omen. Anything to taint his glory. The toilet door had also upset him. Because it was warped, it had jerked open with a sudden thud. He inwardly blamed the Germans and understood that this was why he'd telephoned the museum again. The train swooshed past a clump of metal stacking chairs, each bent into the next.

Everything was in order, of course. Preparations were paramount when transporting such an old and fragile artefact, not to mention a potentially dangerous one, if history was to be believed. And why should it not be? Why should we not believe it? Why bother creating a golem, if one didn't believe? No, there was too much literature to ignore. Clammy emotional logic was useless here, although Max acknowledged his fierce feelings for the find. Cold angular insight was called for. Dispense with fancy pivots of phrase. A large room off the Main Hall had been emptied of other, now poor-relation exhibits, and the temperature lowered to match that of the garrett of the French church in which he had found the golem. Hydraulic lifting equipment was waiting, with clamps open for its cargo, on the station platform.

Max glanced at his watch, a very fine imitation IWG 1999. It was 10.22. Still some time to go. The lateness of the hour had been a factor in the choosing of this train, but there had probably been nothing to worry about. People look away when they see uniformed guards, or they do in Germany, and four were sat on little folding chairs in Luggage, with the box, and another one in every carriage of the train.

He relaxed and took a folder that had been prepared by the museum from his briefcase. He knew everything it contained, but wanted to gaze at the ghastly thing for luck. It had lenticular covers. The gaudy holographic plates of plastic you sometimes see sandwiching fashion magazines. He felt it reel beneath his violent smile. There were several depictions of golems that gyrated when you moved the folder from side to side. He thought it vaguely pornographic, and was scandalised by the use of colour — everyone knows golems are always rendered in black-and-white, or they should. He was damned if this aberration was going to be circulated at the lecture/press-conference scheduled for three days hence. Life's repetitive minutiae — when would they learn?

Vulgar, foul, insulting, it reminded him of the films he used to watch as a faithless teenager. They were called "the pictures" then.

There was one that was all the rage in Europe. Set predominantly on a baseball pitch in the US of A, it told the story of a lesbian coach who had a phobia of tiered-stalls, or bleachers. In fact, it became clear, she was frightened of bleachers *because* she was lesbian. Such idiocy! Such wanton unsurprising blasphemy.

Nausea rose again, quiet but secure. His eyes grew narrow as squeaks. *What business did lenticular covers have when it came to the solemn history of golems? My life has been just such a solemn history. I am more bearable to myself when asleep.*

With nothing to do but wait, he opened the front cover, flipped a few pages of preliminary publishing info, and read:

Introduction

In Jewish tradition, the golem is a recurring yahoo.

Good line, I'll give you that, he thought.

It most often occurs as an artificial creature created by magic, often to serve the creator in any of one to three ways. It is thought the three wishes of the genie are descended from this. The word 'golem' appears only once in the Bible (Psalms 139:16) [see appendix 1]. In Hebrew it most often means 'shapeless mass', although the Talmud uses the word in other ways, including 'imperfect' or 'unformed'. According to Talmudic legend, Adam [see appendix 2] is called 'golem', meaning 'body without a soul' (Sanhedrin 38b) for the first twelve hours of his existence. The figure of the golem also appears in other places in the Talmud [see appendix 3]. One legend states that the prophet Jeremiah created a golem. However, some mystics believe the creation of a golem has symbolic meaning only, such as a spiritual experience following a religious rite.

Yeah, well, that's *going to take a beating*, he thought, *when they see what I've got to offer. And three* oftens *in one paragraph? These people are idiots. Why would a mystic disbelieve anything?* Professor Fellrain smiled and read on:

The Sefer Yetzirah ('Book of Creation') [see appendix 4], often thought of as a guide to the use of magic by many Western

131

European Jews in the Middle Ages, gives instructions on how to create a golem. Many of their versions share shaping the golem into a figure resembling a human form and of using God's name to bring it to life, since God is the ultimate creator of life ...

Professor Fellrain yawned. *These imbeciles,* he thought, *I'm the only brain in the department worth a damn. Look at them wrestling with the basics, while I make history.* He skipped forward a page.

Ashkenazi Hasidic Jewish lore states that the golem would often come to life and serve its creator or creators by doing tasks assigned to it. By far the most famous instance of the golem is connected to Rabbi Judah Loew ben Bezalel, the Maharal of Prague (1513 – 1609) [see appendix 7]. It is said that he created a golem from clay to protect the Jewish community from Blood Libel and to help out doing physical labour, since golems possess legendary strength. Other versions claim that it was close to Easter, 1580, and a Jew-hating priest was attempting to incite the Christians against the Jews. Thus the golem's role was to protect the Jewish community during the Easter festivities.

Really? he thought. *This is getting less and less good.*

Both versions recall the golem running amok and threatening innocent lives, so Rabbi Loew removed the Divine Name, rendering the golem lifeless. A separate account has the golem going mad and running away. Several sources attribute the story to Rabbi Elijah of Chelm [see appendix 8], saying Rabbi Loew, one of the most outstanding Jewish scholars of the sixteenth century, who wrote numerous books on Jewish law, philosophy and morality, would have actually opposed the creation of a golem.

He hated scholars who presumed to understand the workings of a Godly life. They were more irritating than scientists. And the golem running away ... *Pah. Unsubstantiated, yes, and ridiculous.* Smoothing his jacket uneasily over his hips, he continued:

The golem has been a popular figure in the arts in the past few centuries with both Jews and non-Jews. In the early twentieth century several plays, novels, musicals, movies and even a ballet were based on the golem [see appendix 9]. The most famous works where golems appear are Mary Shelley's *Frankenstein*, Karel Capek's *R.U.R.* (where the word 'robot' comes from), Issac Bashevis Singer's *The Golem*, Michael Chabon's *The Amazing Adventures of Kavalier and Clay*, and episodes of the popular American TV show *The X-Files*. There is also a character named Golem in Tolkein's classic *The Lord Of The Rings*. Today, there is even a golem museum in the Jewish Quarter of Prague [see appendix 10]. It is recommended visiting it if you find yourself in that wonderful city. Sometimes, someone who is large but intellectually slow is called a golem. Other civilisations, such as the ancient Greeks, have similar concepts.

Yes, he thought — that's *about right. Ironically, I've been surrounded by golems my entire working life. Atomic cripples.* He almost laughed, but caught it in time. The Professor was a man who generally laughed as little as possible. *Twenty years of non-stop work, with little professional recognition, and they talk about Sci-Fi TV.* The dull blue baubles of his eyes flicked up to a sky the colour of cuttlefish ink. He could almost smell it. The damp pong of German nights.

(The word *Abracadabra*, incidentally, derives from *avra k'davra*, Aramaic for 'I create as I speak.') Thus, under the rarest of circumstances, a human being may imbue lifeless matter with that intangible, but essential spark of life: the soul. The Kabbalists [see appendix 11] saw the creation of a golem as a kind of alchemical task, the accomplishment of which proved the adept's skill and knowledge of Kabbalah (Jewish mysticism). In popular legend, however, the golem became a kind of folk hero. Tales of mystical rabbis creating life from dust abounded, particularly in the Early Modern period, and inspired such tales as *Frankenstein* and *The Sorcerer's Apprentice*. Sometimes the golem saves the Jewish community from persecution or death [see appendix 12], enacting the kind of heroism or revenge unavailable to powerless Jews. Often, however, Jewish folktales [see appendix 13] about the golem tell what happens when things go awry — when the power of life-force goes astray, often with tragic results.

The waiter/ess/other approached, bearing a telephone on a tray. 'Professor Fellrain, a call for you.'

He picked up the receiver. It was his research assistant. 'Indeed, yes. *Yes.* The lecture is on Friday. You get in by noon? Fine. Go straight to the hotel and pick up my notes. Yes, it will be an extraordinary day. You have the details. *I* don't know. Didn't we stay there last time? A leafy place, I think. Dr Tav Singh recommended it. I remember him saying he met H. R. Giger there one year ...'

A cold wind suddenly rushed through the train, interrupting the grey wefts of his hair. The telephone line was dead. Receiver idling between shoulderblade and chin, Professor Max Fellrain looked up. There was no one else in the dining car. The Jew/ess/other had vanished, although he noticed a bell on the wall to call him/her/they if needed. From where? He hoped he/she/they was/were rotting away inside, some intellectual or spiritual maggot, starved of sustenance, gorging itself to the surface skin. Skin is all. A race to the skin.

The train was passing some kind of excavation site, or perhaps the conception of a quarry — mounds of earth were silhouetted, pile by pile by pile, stone by stone by stone. The brakes had been gently applied. No need to be alarmed. No need to press that bell. *Yet* — 23.06 — there were to be no unscheduled stops. That had been agreed with the company. Then there was a loud clanging, as of a torture instrument, and the brakes tightened till the train juddered. No question: they were stopping. Professor Fellrain realised he felt afraid, then instantly dismissed the feeling as absurd. You must, as when flying in an aeroplane, dismiss the fear. The mind rising above. A billiard of phlegm rattled around his lungs. Bile in the stomach.

He got out of his seat and walked briskly to the end of the dining car in the direction he gauged the clang to have come from. There were three people visible — an elderly gentleman with a curved hat and sad violinists' eyes, who didn't seem bothered by the commotion, and a mother and child. They *were* bothered, the child bawling and batting at its mother. She was a threadbare woman, who kept turning from the hips to gaze dully down the carriage. If, as he'd always believed, children wanted one parent to be slow, in order to make the world more accessible, then this woman was assuredly that parent. He felt contempt for her rising in his chest like heartburn, when the whole train began to rock with what felt like the drumskin rumble of military boots. No longer afraid, and sensing something brown and evil inside him, Max opened the joining carriage door and began to run toward the sound. He had to wrestle past several passengers running in the opposite direction, but paid no attention. The mind must focus. Cold thought.

Three carriages down he saw the golem. It was lumbering through, bending the steel grab rails as it advanced, cracking the tough plastic backs of seats and sending flat cushions skittering. It left indentations in the floor as it went, and this was causing the train's rocking. It seemed to be searching for something, shifting to and fro. The Professor stepped forward, arms open. If I'm going to go, he thought, I'll go embracing G-d. He closed his eyes.

135

After some long seconds, during which a ragged breeze drainpiped up his trousers and momentarily froze his penis, he opened them again.

'You summoned me. What would you have me do?'

Professor Max Fellrain, cowering beneath a shattered buckled window, could only gawp for a moment. Regaining his wits, he coughed with reddened cheeks: 'You can *talk*?'

'Do not believe everything you are told and have read. Only you can see and hear me. How should I address you?'

This augured well. Manners are the basis of society, and if the thing could talk, never mind *be polite*, it was all to the good. Hell, it would be his legacy, his legend!

'I am Professor Maximilian Fellrain,' he said. 'You may address me as Max. Are we ... friends?'

This last question he added cautiously, since the golem was an intimidating specimen. Although in its inanimate form it had had no discernible neck, now animated its head creakily pivoted, slightly out of time with the rest of its body. It smelled tatty and bestial to Fellrain's turbulent nostrils, yet he had to admit that the being possessed a clunky charm, if not elegance.

'I do not know what friends are, Max. If you are my master you must tell me what you would have me do.'

The mind must focus. Cold thought.

'How should I address you?' he countered.

'That does not matter.'

Tentatively stepping forward, he offered: 'Are you *my* golem?'

'This also does not matter.'

'May I touch you?'

'As you wish.'

The Professor reached up and touched the creature over where the heart should have been. Through his fingertips he felt little alive pulses everywhere, not only in the fingertips but his body and the air around. He felt instantly vulnerable, let down by everything he'd ever cared about. It was a fully crushing feeling. He imagined he felt like a woman. Tears poured from his eyes. Let them come, permit them. His dreams were trex.

'I'm sorry, I'm so sorry,' he sobbed, 'I never understood ...'

136

'I do not understand *sorry*, nor does it matter. You must tell me what you would have me do.'

The golem shuffled back a step, almost louchly, giving room to speak or think. It flensed, contracted, as if trying to formulate intelligence. At length Max said: 'I have spent my life looking for you. Not only my working life, but my whole life. You have been a dream since my childhood. I wanted you to exist more than I even imagined possible. You have been my life. What *can* I say?'

'This does not matter, Max.'

Time had crumbled to grey powder. External human shouts registered, far away, but were meaningless. The golem's appearance had changed, he suddenly noticed. It now had a pronounced underbite. The hands shimmered. And had its lips even moved when it spoke? Pockets of midges eddied about its head.

'Okay. I found you and I want to show you to the world. You're mine. I want you to bring me adulation. *Fame*. You're mine.'

'Fame you will certainly have, Max, but I cannot help you attain it. Remember also that fame, as you put it, is fleeting in most cases. Including yours.'

'What do you mean?'

'I mean exactly what I say. Your fame will be fleeting.'

'But I will have fame?'

'Certainly. It is yours. But Max, this is not what I am here for. You did not create me. There is no emotional connection. It is merely what it is. Time is drawing in. What would you truly have me do?'

From the golem's various junctures, knees, shoulders, ankles, steam had begun purling up, as if from subterranean recesses.

'Help me,' he said, 'show me the way to true Godliness. *That's* why I brought you here. Make me near to Him.' The Professor's voice was quivering. He didn't fully understand it himself. The golem stepped forward.

'Max, I cannot help you with this. You must tell me precisely what you would have me do.'

'I can't,' he sobbed. 'Just get back in the box and let me take you to the Museum. I need you to to be real, tangible, but not like this …'

'Do you wish me to leave you now?'

'No. You must stay and make my reputation. You must. Remember the *fame*. It's overwhelming ...' There was a pause. Then, with the indifference of one who can better control a situation the worse off he is, the Professor added: 'Oh, I don't care. You're a *fake*. A fraud. What face are you showing?'

The golem disappeared. Powder on the floor. Grey mist.

Desolation overcame him and he passed out. Distant bells, sirens, and much swearing. Passengers herded out. A SWAT-team swinging down on ropes, spotlights pinned.

Where the hell was his briefcase? He'd need that, he knew.

* * * *

Max's fame was fleeting, of course.

The train — carriages ripped up, seats torn asunder — made the news, the damage somehow attributed to drug-crazed youths from a local music festival, who had all disappeared before emergency response units arrived on the scene. TV interviews made him a laughing-stock. Not really listening, or understanding if they were, what he was trying to say about 'his golem', viewers seemed to think the Professor was claiming to have 'hulked out' and caused the damage to the train himself. No trace could be found of the 'uniformed guards' he babbled about, and the Swiss government simply denied their existence and forbade him from ever setting foot on Swiss soil again. The German and French governments swiftly followed suit. Labelled 'a fiasco' in the press — they were uneasy with "disaster" since no one had visibly or provably died — the 'freak train' was soon forgotten. But Fellrain's reputation was irreparably tarnished, and he stayed a laughing-stock.

Many of the people on the train made good copy though — the man with sad violinists' eyes gave a long interview with a focus on Sufism entitled *Have Two Wings With Which To Fly Down The Path Of Love Not One*. I heard he turned the experience into a bestselling book the following year. Good for Old Melancholy Eyes. The woman-with-child's interview — him screaming in tongues, her mortally confused — became one of the most played on Swiss and

German funny-clip shows over the following months, until displaced by a schoolgirl falling on her face while pole-dancing.

Many years later, after he had been stripped of his Professorship and was working as a manicurist in a shop called *The Tweezer Place*, Maxy met a woman. She was a skinny, shallow-fleshed Jewess with steel spectacles, who'd never heard of his past. He ascertained this first. She was a serene person, who assumed it in others: a serenity of mind. Her life was a chain of disappointments, but she didn't make any connections. Nor should she have. Maxy was bound to be the next. It seems that happiness is often resigning oneself to repetition and hoping to find variety.

They moved into a small house together in Vienna, surrounded by a *Fatsia japonica* hedge, which he trimmed three times a year. His smiles were not often so spiteful. She had ample thighs and liked to wear tights. Maxy heard a *frish* whenever she passed. These days he looked like a man who wore earplugs in bed. Careful, systematic, German. He didn't have time for any of this. Whenever he thought of the golem he felt only sadness, and perhaps a little pity. For himself? Who would ever know? He overspent in his imagination. Running up bills on useless fripperies.

I am more intelligent, more humane, when I am asleep, dreaming, he thought. Let me go to dreams. Even if the sleep be fitful, let me dive back in. You won't miss me when I'm gone. This is not to say that he wanted to die, only that disillusionment breeds indifference.

One day the Jewess, his wife, said to him:

'Why do you never call me by my actual name?'

Because I hate you, he thought, and the life I'm forced to live.

He didn't say that out loud of course. The ex-professor had learned his lesson. He considered it a harsh one, but he had learned it. After deliberation, he answered:

'Because I hate you, my dear, and the life I'm forced to live. You smell bad too.'

Oh dear, oh dear, Maxy, would he ever learn? Giggles for the full condition. The full condition is all. Skin be damned. Jewishness too, he felt.

Last night outside the salon he saw a pair of grotty foxes

frotting viciously on a car bonnet. Enough with the pivots of phrase.

The full condition isn't a box of nothingness. It's a full box. Time is merely the ribbon wrapped around it.

Diary from a War Zone

Across the rooftops some man sings melancholy songs. The sound fills me like hope. And hope is a good thing. Perhaps the best thing. 'Come on over,' I want to shout. 'I know those little songs.' But his music is loud. He can't hear. He certainly can't hear me.

Walk close to the wall. The wind will not blow cold there.

Anand is such a wonderful boy. He's younger than me, but none of that matters anymore. At least he's not shorter: ha. Small things bring smiles. He told me his mother used to say: 'Bread is the staff of life'.

Eighteen months ago I'd have found that mildly funny. Now, at least since everything went to crap and the army moved in and took control, it's bloody hilarious. What I wouldn't give for some bread. Or at least a cigarette to take the want away.

I'm not saying it's going to be easy. I'm saying it's going to be worth it.

Random thoughts but with singular purpose.

Oh Leise, Leise, my mother. Nearly a week gone. The house still smells of you. Daddy cries, upstairs. He drinks vodka by the bottle, when we can procure it.

  Leise, your sorrowful name made more sorrowful since the bastards killed you out on the corner. 3.2 minutes after curfew. In the street. Oh mummy, mummy, why did it have to be this way? We begged you not to go. Leise, Leise, *pace* now.

  Where's a cigarette to take the pain away?

3 a.m. The usual patrols. I wasn't sleeping anyway. With all the searchlights idly making eerie geometric shapes in the sky, we found out over a year ago that curtains were pointless. Best just get used to it. Anyway, if they want to enter your house, they will. I

can't believe I used to find uniformed men attractive. Since Exodus Time, all I see are unmasked brutes. Under any sky.

I play games on my own. The fate of pawns bothers me. The outside, the conflict, affects everything, down to the most inconsequential detail. I used to love the boardgame Campaign, where each player chose a country — Russia, Austria, Prussia, France, Spain or Italy — and attacked or made truces with the others. The three different types of piece denoted infantry, cavalry and an Emperor (or Empress I used to think) for each place. Set during the Napoleonic era, it hugely appealed to a schoolgirl obsessed with military history. But now — I can't even bear to look at the box. I even worry about pawns in my sleep.

Boredom.

Just music. Only music. But quietly, of course. No sane person wants to attract attention here.
  We have an actual streetsweep.

Today I tried on a turquoise T-shirt mummy bought me when I was seventeen. I shouldn't only talk about the past, but memories are what we have now. It's where we seek to live. Anyway, it still fitted — mostly. But won't for much longer: ha. It's properly old-school, with an embroidered pink and white thistle-y flower design diagonally across it. Oh, how it's soft and featherly. I found an old blue skirt too, that I hadn't seen in ages. It was smocked at the waist! I could hardly believe it. Cute.
  Five people's throats were slit on our road this morning.
  That's what days are like now — the endless riffling through things, I mean, not the belief bit, or the being surprised bit.
  Surprise is not a feature of Exodus Time, since its very basis is unbelievable, or not believable.
  Or not believable to us secret non-believers.
  Or to the sane.

What the hell. I should find my guitar. I think it's in the basement.

There are some good new songs on the radio I could try and learn. I can re-write the lyrics. I'm not singing *those* words, however nice the music is.

We hear that 12 people were beheaded on Brudenell Road at sundown last night.

We thought we heard the chanting.

ET's turned to AA: ha! Listening to the 'press' again. Exodus Time to After Age. What *is* it with all these names? No, all these tags?

We also heard Post-Time (PT I guess) on the radio. Yes ... 'One of the positives of all this,' daddy quipped, in between gulps, 'is that radio has come back in a *big* way'.

TV is pointless now, filled with religious propaganda, repeats deemed appropriate — comedy is obviously banned — and only intermittent and highly dubious news updates.

Besides, there *is* no news. Or no new news. Only emptiness. He's right.

We must think of something. Anand and me and the jellybean. What to do with daddy though?

Anand managed to come round. I hadn't seen him for many days. I wore the turquoise T-shirt, and we both had a quarter-glass of champagne. It's important to hoard things like champagne, choco-late, toilet roll, etc. Things for bartering later. He's a sweet boy and told me crazy tales of huge building projects north of the city and the leaders of the Old World forced to publicly convert, on their knees. Legendising. He claims it's all true, but I know him. And I know it's important to have something to do or say. And almost anything *will* do, in the face of implacable belief.

'I can't stop looking at you,' he said.

Oh no, no, no, no. No. Apparently they've introduced pregnancy licences. This means I have committed a crime. Their Holy Book is 'only of peace'. Their religion is 'a religion of peace'. Since I have already committed a crime I have nothing to lose when I say their religion is racist, misogynist, homophobic, totalitarian, inquisitional, imperialist and genocidal. They have never had a Reformation, and never will now they're fully in charge. Their Holy Book contains many punishments for crimes, but everyone says the most common one now is — they throw you in jail and treat you well. You get fed. You get watered. You must pray at the given times, of course that is compulsory. But you're okay. Then your birthday comes up. They take you out into the main courtyard, where many of the other prisoners can observe. There is a barrel of hot tar and a stool in the centre. After telling you that it is indeed your birthday, they then give you your birthday present. This comes in the form of two questions.

'Top — left or right, or bottom — left or right?'

Then:

'Go high or go low?'

The first question refers to either your right or left arm or your right or left leg. The second question refers to above or below the elbow, or above or below the knee.

Then a guard comes out with a machete, accompanied by a Holy man, and gives you the practical second part of your birthday present.

They say that for female prisoners rape often features too, though I guess this could be the only situation in a woman's life when rape is not the worst thing that could befall her that day. I don't know. I guess it depends. It all always depends.

We've simply got to do something soon. We have to. Death isn't such a big thing anymore. So few worries really, but the main ones. Life is touching our useless fingers.

Anand suggested simply leaving daddy. Says he'll die soon anyway. I understand. And I agree, he will. I don't think any less of Anand for suggesting this course of action. These are everyday decisions.

He's not heartless. And I'm not a bad daughter for considering it. But it doesn't feel, at least not yet, like the correct decision. There has to be some other way. Life was never like this. I must think.

Time isn't a problem. We have lots of that. Lots and lots and lots.

146

Religion absolutely *adores* boredom. It's perhaps all we have, boredom. Trying to live with civil impulses in the heart — humanity at its minimum. Not much left for personal appeal. That's merely lasting, not even surviving. Daddy lasts, but for how much longer? Can we hold on without being found out? He moans all the time. I turn up the music, but not too much. I am a dismal creature. We are all dismal little creatures.

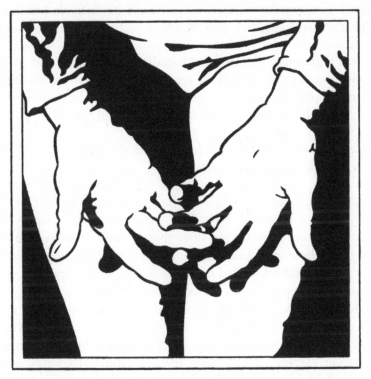

Daddy was always a dependable man. He thought of others and often thought *for* others. Rose up the ranks of his profession quickly. Now he frowns and moans and pleads for more vodka. There are no hints of old noble expressions. I'm sorry to say daddy, but I wish they'd killed you instead of mummy out on the corner. She could have left with us. Oh Leise, Leise. 'Do not weep for me,' she'd say.

I need new air. Or a cigarette.

Tonight there are war sounds. Different from occupation sounds. The tiny sounds of After Age, or whatever era or epoch we're supposed to be in now, never close by. Detonations beyond the rooftops. The man who used to sing melancholy songs no longer sings. Now it's just the saddest song — the bassdrop followed by a brief shrub of smoke. I'm not frightened anymore. But my mind is not yet made up. Where's Anand? I'm gently worried. I haven't heard from him for some days, but I know it's difficult. I wish I had a brother, or even a male cousin, who could accompany me outside.

A bad daddy-day. He's redder than disease, swearing and shaking. I wish I could just suck all the oxygen out of his room and let him silently suffocate in a soundproofed world. Problem solved. Ha. Yes, horrible thoughts are proving easy to find.

After curfew, a leak began somewhere in the house.
I think I've made up my mind.

Daddy's a cypher. In many ways he's already absent. But I should put down something about him here before he's really gone. Exodus Time, or whatever, does that to you — makes one thing fill your whole eyes. Leaving no time for any extra light. Extremities feel tenderised, pulled out. Like making the shape of a snow-angel. Fingertips, toes — the tiny vulnerable human ends.
Mummy and daddy met in Jerusalem thirty-six years ago. I never got to see Jerusalem before it was destroyed. Met in 'a warm and well-lit place' he used to say. Even then he was a man of apparent elegance and certain regular habits. His lungs weren't good — had never been good — but he thought himself happy. His disturbed breathing formed questions into assertions.
After the wedding — in full colour — they returned here, to our city, and poverty. But he began to train as a doctor of the eyes, an ophthalmologist I think it's called (we have no internet anymore to check, and books have been confiscated), and eventually a fair income materialised. Mummy said that while he studied, concentrating hard, bent over books, his lungs would whistle like an asthmatic old woman's.

I came along after five years, and since by then mummy already felt that something had withered in their love, I was the welcome fresh face. Daddy wasn't given to extravagant gestures, preferring calm and even silly ones. But he was a cautious man and demanded absolute silence at night so that, even while sleeping, he could watch over the noises of the house. The squeaks and groans; the archival yaws.

These are the things I remember, daddy.

Oh yes, and he always shaved by touch. I never knew why. It wasn't for lack of a mirror. Perhaps feeling the scratch scratch scratch relaxed him. Perhaps it was merely nostalgia for his own father. Little things can soothe, can turn a day from bad to good. One could be happy here. That I understand.

These are the things I remember, daddy.

But then he began to change. Routine would be forgotten. Former fastidiousness waned. I didn't really notice it, or care I guess, until my late teens. Sometimes a complete picture of our lives would shine in his eyes and then be gone. *Fizz*. A totally unrelated subject announced by a tiny incline of the chin. From time to time he took on false expressions. At a dinner party he'd suddenly look like a bewildered small boy. Looks that didn't correspond to the situation. The way deaf people have of looking at things. They *look*.

These are the things I remember, daddy.

Exasperation grew within him, but he couldn't recognise it, and grew more exasperated for that. One day he retraced every step he'd taken, looking for lost coins. Mummy said he'd talk for hours on the alarming state of his intestines. In my twenty-year-old life, there was an empty space of daddy's perfect size and shape.

Unsettlingly tranquil movements.

Speaking as if with a gravelly sediment on the tongue. Then his speech began to contain incoherencies — full adult sentences with one false quantity. 'Don't worry sweetie, your college fund is in fine fettle, I made sure of that, but why is there a fly in your eye?'

By this stage there was enough hair on his hands to account for

what had fallen off his head.
Daddy, I remember.

Anand is back and he has a plan. Or so he thinks. *Escape*. Ha. It could work. And even if it doesn't, we'll be free for a little while. A little while is better than never having tried at all, I guess. We could still come through — stumbling, faltering, but clear. Perhaps. And perhaps be damned.

But … horrible thoughts. The problem of daddy. I cannot take him. This is obvious. I am a dismal evil thing. But daddy would understand. Fungus in his innards. He would understand for the jellybean, or so I tell myself. He would understand not wanting to be just a torso and a head, with another birthday coming up. Our *religion of peace*. And what a darkly funny oxymoron that is: that any religion could be one of peace. Ha. I tell myself this every minute. I remember, daddy, I *do*. I will always remember. That's why I need a cigarette. Badly. The less air the better.

I found the guitar. To remember mummy, tonight I sang: Liza, Liza, skies are grey / But if you smile at me, all the clouds will roll away / Liza, Liza, don't delay / Come keep me company, and the clouds will roll away …

Name the day. When you belong to me.
    Daddy, all the clouds will roll away.
    I will always remember you.
    Everything will look as it always did. Everything will be warm. I really need a cigarette for this. Anand, wherever you are, please bring some smokes.

The world will touch your fingers and the world will touch your toes. The world will do things I can't, daddy, because it's so big and I'm so small.
    How ironic — for a second it struck me that there is no reason left to *not* believe. Useless thoughts. A military strobe light just cut the house in two. I wonder if you somehow saw it, in your sleep, with those retreating eyes that caused so many others to clearly see.

I'm in your room now, daddy. Your door opened with a slight *frish*. You gave slightly to my nudge — a recollection? Some still-wired part of the brain that is forever linked to your daughter's touch? There has to be something. There just has to be something. But I wonder if humans are ready for reality. And who am I to tell them? Ha.

I must consolidate.

I must change tense.

But you're still asleep. I could recognise that breathing anywhere. Not an old woman's anymore, but a complex study of wheezing counterpoint. A fugue played on a harmonium whose pedal hasn't been pumped in a few minutes. And a few minutes is all it will take, daddy. I promise.

I use those plastic ties you bought for the garden trellis to join your arms to the rails on the sides of the bed.

The tenses are confusing.

I brush my tears from your cheeks and take the pre-soaked towel. It's not daddy anymore, I tell myself, as I press down and hold and hold and hold. Hours seem to slip down their flagpoles. How long have I been holding on? I still hold on. To hell with the lot of you. To hell with what the world will think. Name the day, Leise. When you belong to me.

Each second ticks past pizzicato.

Will it ever stop raining? Love's a big illusion. Let's hear it for that other famous lie: Love makes the world go round. Ha. And ha. And ha ha ha ha ha. Was daddy wrong in what he tried to do? Were we? Ferry me down. But hold, hold. Hold.

It is done and I burst into life. Where is Anand? Death is a powerful insigator of erotic scenarios. I need Anand from now on, here, now. I should try to sleep. But I feel like a pile of stones. Tomorrow has not yet begun. Dawn has a pleasant precision.

Hello me. Good morning. Feel good about you. I can't risk taking this diary of course, so I'm leaving this for whoever finds it. Whoever does will probably instantly burn it anyway, as a devil's piece. But goodbye daddy. Remember that I loved you. Remember that I cared.

Anand's here now, and saying we must leave.

Yes, yes, we must. We will.

So, I put down my last words here.

Daddy, you once told me a story about how you left a note on my mum's door while you were first dating — so, on *her* mother's door. Your future mother-in-law, ha. You wrote three lines:

Will be [where we arranged to meet]

Wait for [a pickup point]

Want to [tell you I love you?]

Who knows? But Leise's mother tore the sellotaped note from the door, ripped it down the middle. She never noticed, as she screwed up the paper in her hand, that she had left a portion still attached to the door. The portion left read

Will be

Wait for

Want to

And that fragment of a note, 30-odd-years-old, is what I'll take with me. The only connection now between us — me, you, daddy upstairs.

We're going now. Heading into a future and hoping the clouds will roll away. I hope to hear some guy singing again. I hope. And hope is a good thing.

We'll come through — I *believe* it. And may be coming through will be some amazing accomplishment. Not all accomplishments have to be admirable, or even moral. And may be nothing has been accomplished.

Titbits with Williams

All the way back in 1970, a local drunk (commonly known as Porky) broke into a trailer and stole a jug of moonshine. Porky was infamous for stealing booze thereabouts, occasionally at knife-point, but on this particular occasion he'd bitten off more than he could chew. He'd crossed the line. That was *it*. The enraged owner — who we can be sure had been brewing said moonshine for some time — grabbed his rifle and kicked in the door of Porky's trailer to retrieve the pilfered hooch. He discovered Porky drinking with their buddy Bennie Lightsy. A scuffle ensued during which Bennie was shot dead.

This might have been an everyday American tragedy, had not the shooting happened at a scientific research station located on an ice floe in the Arctic Ocean.

The station was supposedly researching climate patterns, but in hindsight it sounds more like an exercise in how far one can push a laboratory technician before he snaps and attempts to marry a polar bear. The nineteen scientists and technicians were stationed in unimaginable conditions — or perhaps I just don't want to — for months at a time, entirely isolated from the civilised world, with nothing to do but drink and listen to the base's two eight-track tapes. Since one of the tapes was a Jefferson Airplane one, they soon went understandably crazy. Porky had descended into fulmi-nant alcoholism, and had indeed attacked another scientist with a meat cleaver in order to filch their stash. This all culminated in researcher Mario Escamilla accidentally shooting his boss Bennie Lightsy, while trying to recover that aforementioned jug of pruno.

However, since the shooting took place on an ice floe in international waters, it was technically impossible for any nation to prosecute Dr Escamilla. There are laws that allow for crimes committed on *vessels* to be prosecuted, but an iceberg isn't a vessel in any legal sense, no matter how big it is, or how many scientists have vomited on it.

But as it turned out, the United States was able to find an ingenious solution to the problem. By ignoring it completely.

American law enforcement eventually gave up on trying to find a legal loophole and simply sent a plane out to the ice floe to grab Escamilla and take him back to Virginia. Happy days. The unusual circumstances meant that the subsequent trial was technically illegal, but the issue was never resolved because the rifle turned out to have a faulty trigger and the jury acquitted Dr Escamilla on the grounds that he had probably never intended to discharge the weapon at all.

This convenient solution allowed everyone to go back to ignoring the problem. At least until an astronaut develops space madness. Then we'll have to put together an elite force of astro-cops to catch the intergalactic mangler. Perhaps Elon Musk has that covered.

There is no record of what became of Porky.

* * * *

There was once a gannet named Nigel. For those unfamiliar with such things, a gannet is a white bird with a long bill, vibrant yellow neck and head, and with a splash of expensive black feathers toward its rear.

Nigel died in January 2018. May he rest in peace. He was notable for two reasons, a scientific one and an emotional one. He was a beautiful creature who had been lured to a strange place by humans. All alone, he spent years directing his mating instincts toward a false love interest: a painted decoy, eternally oblivious to his wooing. He was in love with a statue. Years passed, no other gannets arrived, and there Nigel died, alone with his princess of cement.

Yet conservationists did not mourn his fate. Nigel, they claim, was a hero among gannets — a veritable avian saint — a tragic hero, of course, but still a hero.

Stephen Kress, vice president of bird conservation at the National Audubon Society said: 'He was a pioneering spirit. Was he a brave pioneer or a foolish pioneer? I would think of him as a brave pioneer, because it isn't easy to live on the edge like that.' Or indeed on the ledge of rock that he did.

Dr Kress knows about being a pioneer. In the early 1970s he came up with the idea of using decoys and recorded birdcalls to attract seabirds to islands. He was attempting to re-establish a colony of Atlantic puffins on Eastern Egg Rock, a Maine island where hunters had wiped the birds out a century before. But the method he employed — moving chicks to the island and hoping they'd come back to nest there — didn't work. They didn't come back. Then Dr Kress underwent an astounding encephalisation.

'It kind of hit me one day that the thing that was missing for this highly social bird, that always nests in colonies, was others of its kind. I put out some decoys and almost immediately puffins started appearing.' He also broadcast puffin calls, because puffins are notoriously vocal. And he put out strategically placed mirrors, because although the puffins were savvy enough to lose interest in an immobile model, they were apparently fooled into believing their reflections were peers. As of summer 2017, Eastern Egg Rock was home to 172 puffin breeding pairs. And Dr Kress's method, known as Social Attraction, is now used worldwide to start, or re-start, seabird colonies on islands.

Including New Zealand, where gannets are not endangered, but only clustered in a few obscure places. Wildlife experts would like them to be 'more geographically diverse', said Chris Bell, a conservation ranger who is the sole human inhabitant of Mana Island, where Nigel — remember him? — made his home.

Mana was deemed a good site for a gannet Social Attraction project because invasive predators had been eradicated, and because the birds, with their fertilising guano, could help 'restore the kind of ecosystem [the island] had before humans arrived', he wrote in an email to your humble author.

Yet such projects depend on birds that defy their deep instincts to return to their birthplace — a process or tendency known as philopatry. In other words, success depends on Nigels, and those like him. Let's hear it for the little guy. Except there aren't any others quite like Nigel.

'Without birds like Nigel, there wouldn't be any new colonies. The species would be locked into this philopatric pattern ...'

leaving it vulnerable to wipeouts caused by introduced predators or rising sea levels or illness. Dr Kress — remember him? — continued: '[Nigel is] a hero! He gave it all for the species. He tried.'

The Mana project began in the late 1990s, when schoolchildren first began painting the gannet decoys, but it was not until 2015 that a real one — Nigel — showed up. By staying, Mr Bell claimed, Nigel acted as an unintentional living advertisement for the spot. Shortly before Nigel's demise, after Bell and his colleagues moved the speakers playing gannet calls closer to the decoy colony, three more gannets showed up. Nigel exhibited no interest in them — the live birds. He loved his stone companion and that was that. Perhaps he had better hearing than others.

Gannets 'like to see that other birds have gone there, before they trust a place. The three regular birds we currently have are Nigel's legacy.'

Despite the isolation, Mr Bell said that New Zealand conservation officials never considered relocating Nigel. Gannets are known to fly thousands of miles between New Zealand and Australia; Mana Island is located two miles from New Zealand's North Island.

Bell added: 'Nigel was a free agent.' His infatuation with a decoy 'was odd behaviour for a gannet, but every group has their individuals.' A trailblazer. A star.

Many seabirds attracted to islands by decoys leave early on, said Dr Kress. Nigel may simply have seen advantages in Mana that his fellow gannets did not. A sense of peace, a lack of crowds, a strife-free relationship. All clear advantages, I'd wager.

'Either they're going to attract other members of their kind, or they'll give up and they'll leave. Nigel could have done either of those things. But time caught up with him ...'

And time waits for no one. Perhaps Nigel didn't like crowds. Perhaps Nigel suffered from mental-health problems, or was understandably, and stunningly, sane. Perhaps he really did love his cement bride, and no one else would do.

But please remember Nigel, nestling next to his statue lover, year after year, until he eventually died there. Unloved, except by her, with her hard heart and loyal ways. A true fable for our time, perhaps.

I will never know.

* * * *

When one finds oneself, of an evening, musing on questions such as: If every human being died at exactly the same time, would anyone care? and Is your Birth Certificate really your first participation reward? you know it's time for bed, even if that's the least desirable direction the evening could take. And what could be more agreeable than a late night snifter with an American friend? You might have had a hard lonely day, and found your mind drifting to: Can one ever face backwards on a staircase? or Is every broken clock actually telling us when it died, or was murdered by a hungover human?

The other night, I found myself considering the strange conundrum facing historians. Historians of the past have faced the problem of finding the truth with few available facts, and historians of the future will have to find the truth with far too many available facts. Their jobs will entail the additional task of sifting the fake news out, to locate the actual.

Writers ought to enjoy research. If they claim not to, then their stuff probably isn't worth much attention, at least in the genre of fiction. A big part of the writing process is finding oneself *too interested to do anything else*. The great novelist Ian McEwan told me, in a once-swanky bar in Notting Hill, now a chic-gastro-ruin, I must unsorrowfully add, over a few glasses of fine wine (for him) and a few unsophisticated lagers (for myself), how he adored the film *The Fly*. The Cronenberg remake of 1986, not the 1958 original. He had written a full script for a sequel that went quite far in Hollywood apparently, and almost got made, before being unfortunately scuppered by some objection to a major plot twist involving twins, by one of the previous movie's stars, Geena Davis and Jeff Goldblum. I shall keep to myself which one. But the point was, he'd had a fantastic time, he said, researching the science, and didn't regret the time wasted actually penning the beast. Cheers to that, I say.

Back to the other night. A friend of mine, a British lady, had recently returned from a long stay in Japan and was frankly gushing about Japanese bathroom-systems, more enthusiastically than I had seen her gush about anything since we had split up as a romantic couple some years previously. Like any sensible man, I am always happy to hear of myself bested by technology, even, I suppose, by that of a latrine.

The history of the bidet, it turned out, but in particular why they never caught on in America, is very interesting. Research beckoned. I followed, with half a mind on the recent global panic-buying of toilet-roll during the Covid-19 Lockdown. The time seemed auspicious.

Considering that every day the world flushes the equivalent of 270,000 trees down the khazi, if the US switched to bidets — that have been moderately common in Europe for many years — it would save a good many trees. And that's what we want, isn't it, in this more eco-minded era?

Many Americans had never heard of, never mind seen, a bidet before the mid-20th century. When their troops went overseas during World War Two, many encountered them for the first time: in brothels. Unfortunately, this had the effect of making US GIs associate bidets with illicit activity. Which in turn precluded mentioning them when they returned home, as acknowledging the existence of bidets could conceivably amount to a confession of having got one's rocks off in a foreign bordello or two. Also, in the bidet's youth, the Americans and British apparently believed that douching was an effective method of birth control, and subsequently associated bidets unfavourably with contraception. Christian guilt writ large. Obviously, neither douching nor bidets were, or ever will be, effective ways of avoiding those pesky pregnancies. In 1936, Norman Haire, an admirable proponent of birth-control, wrote that *the presence of a bidet is regarded as almost a symbol of sin.*

The French invented the bidet in the 1600s. Before that, it was either chamber pots or squatting outside in the snow. Early bidets obviously couldn't spray water jets yet, and were often just ceramic basins featuring artistic designs (presumably to prettify their practical use), set into a wooden frame to ensure they were of sufficient height. The word *bidet* comes from the French word for a small horse. In 1785, the English antiquarian Francis Grose — a salutary name if ever there was one — defined a bidet as *a kind of tub, contrived for ladies to wash themselves, for which purpose they bestride it like a little French pony.* The idea of 'riding the bidet' spread to English-speaking countries. Indeed, it sometimes became interchangeable with its equestrian namesake. In 1863, the English traveller Jonathan Deacon wrote: [...] *while I trotted behind on a little bidet.* I'll second that sentiment.

French royalty quickly adopted the bidet, which in turn became a luxury associated with the aristocracy. Marie Antoinette even had a bidet in prison while awaiting her execution. The British, of course, refused to countenance anything connected to the hedonism of French aristocracy. This racist view of the 'French pony' shaped the American attitude too. When a hotel in Manhattan installed a bidet in 1900, Americans literally took to the streets to protest.

Of course, menstruation has long been a taboo subject, especially among the religious, as has sexual intercourse. Prostitutes used the bidet for hygiene, but women were expected to handle their monthly cycles in private, relying on 'jelly rags' to stay clean. William Buchan, an 18th century physician, lamented that *there are no women in the world so inattentive to this discharge as the English, and they suffer accordingly* ... Strong stuff. Still, as indoor plumbing evolved in the nineteenth century, so did our humble bidet.

Instead of storing bidets in the bedroom next to the chamber pot, Europeans moved them into the bathroom. Shocking. The first of these plumbed bidets required a tap to fill the bowl. And soon they became inexpensive enough for widespread use. John Harvey Kellogg — yes, of *that* Kellogg family — patented an American bidet in 1928. And here we enter the modern age: instead of using a separate basin, Kellogg's design had a small sprayer in the bowl. As Kellogg expounded in his patent application: [...] *the water is delivered effectively against the anal region and at the same time is not likely to be thrown or discharged from the bowl* [...] *The structure has the further advantage of being very simple and economical.*

But alas, Kellogg's bidet never enthused the US market. Perhaps it was to do with the name he gave it — Anal Douche. Oh, deary me, someone ought to have had a word with him about that. Yet Kellogg wasn't the only visionary American who attempted to popularise the humble bidet. In 1964, Arnold Cohen founded The American Bidet Company. A noble name, I'm sure you'll agree. At very least, a salutary one. A hopeful one. And hope is a good thing. Like Kellogg's, Cohen's sitzbath had a spritzer built in. In Cohen's vision the bidet was about *changing the habits of a nation, weaning us off the Charmin.* Charmin toilet paper, the brand leader, had been founded in Wisconsin in 1928. Hell, Cohen even had a customised numberplate made for his Cadillac that read MR BIDET. What a guy. Jewish too: double trouble.

It didn't work. *I installed thousands of …* [my bidets] *… all over the suburbs of New York,* claimed Cohen, *but advertising was a next-to-impossible challenge. Nobody wants to hear about Tushy Washing 101.* Perhaps it was a name problem again. Why didn't anyone have a word with him about it?

Europe wasn't the only continent to embrace the bidet. They are common in South America and Asia today. In fact, nineteenth century Hindus believed stories of Europeans *wiping with paper* were *vicious libel,* because the practice seemed so wrong to them.

Islamic nations had welcomed the bidet as a tool of cleanliness. In 2015, Turkey's Directorate of Religious Affairs announced a new religious ruling (and we can be sure that they didn't do it lightly):

 If water cannot be found for cleansing, other cleansing material can be used. Even though some sources
 deem paper to be unsuitable as a cleansing material, as
 it is an apparatus for writing, there is no problem in
 using toilet paper.

Back to my English lady friend of the other night. In the 1980s the Japanese company Toto introduced a new milestone in bidet technology, or evolution: the washlet.

A luxurious take on the bidet, the washlet — the precursor of that which my ex was raving about — featured a control panel to adjust water pressure, a deodoriser, and the option for seat-warming. The washlet also included a dryer function and remote-controlled precision jets. Unfortunately, due its prohibitive price, the washlet didn't garner the US market, despite its advertising campaign Clean Is Happy. Now that's a slogan one would expect Americans to get behind. By 2007, Toto was selling 1,000,000 washlets every year, just in Japan. It can't have been the name — washlet is almost cute. Someone must have had a word with them about that.

By the mid-twentieth century, when Americans were no longer strangers to travel in Europe, many tried to bring the bidet to the US. But another problem then presented itself. The high cost of bathroom renovations. Most American bathrooms were simply not designed to facilitate both a toilet and a bidet. And because bidets required water fixtures *and* space, their installation could have ended up costing the average American some considerable dollars, alas. Even the washlet would require an electrical outlet not too far from the toilet.

As I mentioned earlier, in March 2020, the Covid-19 pandemic caused many governments, including those of the US and Britain, to impose Lockdowns that caused many millions of civilians to fear a shortage of toilet paper. People began stockpiling, supermarket shelves were empty. But did Americans think of the bidet? Did they hell. They turned to wet wipes, even though, in the long term, wet wipes would be much more expensive, but hey ho.

Invented in the mid-twentieth century, wet wipes were originally intended to be used in the course of changing babies' nappies. Then Americans adopted them for cleaning barbecues. In the early 2000s, companies cashed in and began marketing them as a toilet paper alternative. Sanitise that shit. By 2018, wet wipes had become a $2.8 billion-per-year industry. Environmental groups claimed wet wipes added to ocean pollution, and contributed to the growing problem of *fatbergs*, those huge hideous blockages that clog sewage systems, one of which was discovered in London to be the size of three double-decker buses. City councils pleaded with people to not use them. And wet wipes are not even mentioned in the US Constitution. But still Americans resisted.

Today, out of all European countries, Italy has the best record with bidets. A building law of 2002 states that every Italian home built must have a bidet. Toto's washlet — that has been upgraded to include the things that caused all this talk in the first place —

appears in around 60 percent of all Japanese households and 90 percent of Venezuelan homes boast a bidet.

And what are those extras that began this talk?

In 2008, Google transformed its Mountain View headquarters, California, by fabulously installing the latest washlet in every bathroom and toilet in its 70,000-plus-room complex. That's the new washlet that my ex-girlfriend found so alluring. High-tech, they feature jets, dryers and *wand-cleaning,* and of course all the other things mentioned earlier in this piece. TechCrunch dubbed them *space toilets*, although I would have gone with Wand Wafters. Unfortunately, Google's decision seemed to reinforce the American idea that bidets are playthings of the elite. I asked several American friends to comment. They said: *Bloody wanker, that's what I would expect* and *Dude, are you serious?* and the pert, yet pertinent, *oh fuck off, Williams.* Fair enough.

I still haven't got round to asking why my ex-girlfriend found *wand-cleaning* such an improvement. I really ought to.

* * * *

So. I found myself, after a conversation with one of those afore-mentioned American friends, thinking about First Ladies. My friend had said something along the lines of how he disliked Michelle Obama, a lady whom I modestly admired. Research, once again, was required. So here are some things I learned about the position.

There seems to be an image of the *First Lady* as being somehow subservient. To the country, to the office, to the husband. In fact, although the position is largely ceremonial, First Ladies are won-derfully important, and ought to be celebrated. But first, some facts.

First Ladies (and everyone in their families) are forbidden from opening a window — of a house, of a car, of a hotel. Nada. Nix. After her time as a First Lady, Obama said, when asked what she missed most about civilian life: *I look forward to getting in a car and rolling down the window and just letting the air hit my face. I mean, I haven't been in a car with the windows open in about seven years if you can imagine that. So I'm gonna* [sic] *spend that first year just hanging out the window.* We sympathise, sigh, and remember what Betty Ford and Eleanor Roosevelt went through to further their charitable goals. Let's not forget Nancy Reagan, who was widely portrayed as a Machiavellian figure behind her husband's presidency. To be fair, by that time, Ronald, like Donald, had ceased to make much sense.

Even though the position is publicly prominent, none are paid for their time. This may seem obvious, but if I was the Prime Minister's First Bloke, say, I'd expect a salary to go with doing the country's bidding. But then I don't have staff. The First Lady has staff. She also has clothing designers who work out what outfits best befit certain occasions. Okay, their rent and lodgings are paid for. According to Marketplace *the President and First Lady pay for their food, parties, vacations, butlers, housekeepers, ushers* ... [at Ritz Carlton rates] ... and Ronald Reagan put it this way: 'You know, with the First Lady, the government gets an employee fee. They have her just about as busy as they have me'. Which is perfect. People adore symmetry and misogyny. It's like the old joke: Q. Why are women always paid less than men? A. Because a woman's work is never done.

Still, at least she gets the same level of protection as her husband. Not so. Research rears its head again. Eleanor Roosevelt was codenamed Rover by the security services allocated to ensure her safety. Nancy Reagan was Rainbow. Jackie Kennedy was Lace. Pat Nixon was Starlight. Michelle Obama was Renaissance. Melania Trump is Muse. Let's take a moment on those codenames. We immediately grasp Lace and Rover. I would hope most people got Starlight. The Obama codename was because something new was happening, but Reagan's was because of Hollywood, where she and her husband had both been stars, and not, as people seem to believe, because of Star Wars, the missile defence system, or the film. And Muse? Muse is by far my favourite. Melania used to be a model of course, and the images are only one click away. But a muse is also a person (or personified source) of inspiration for a creative artist, and in mythology the Muses were nine goddesses, daughters of Zeus and Mnemosyne, who preside over the arts and sciences. I like to think the security services had a laugh with that one. Not at her expense, but at Donald's.

As the Ethics in Government Act of 1978 ruled, a presidential spouse cannot accept gifts that are ... *valued over a certain amount* [...] *all gifts and their values must be declared and are considered property of the US government. In the case made of gifts by friends or close associates* [the First Lady is ...] *given the opportunity to purchase the items by paying the government the estimated value.*

Dolley Madison helped orphans. Mary Todd Lincoln stood up for former slaves and injured soldiers. Betty Ford raised breast cancer-awareness, spoke out in support of the Equal Rights Amendment, and set up the now famous centres for the treatment of addictions. What a gal.

Still, it seems to be an indistinct position. Overt political activity is frowned upon. First Ladies are expected to champion causes they hold dear. Nancy Reagan coined Just Say No, a fractured anti-drug idea, Melania Trump has announced an attack on cyber-bullying, Michelle Obama half-heartedly encouraged kids to eat healthy meals.

But what *is* a First Lady? Yes, wife of the president. But not always ... President Martin Van Buren — a widower, I'll grant you — chose his daughter-in-law to act as the White House Hostess. And many 'insiders' (such as Stephanie Winston Wolkoff — what *is* it with these names?) have suggested that Trump's First Lady is not his wife Melania, but rather his daughter Ivanka, something that is looking increasingly likely — if uncomfortable — to be true.

Melania Trump set tongues wagging when she elected to spend the majority of her time as First Lady in an apartment in New York, rather than Washington. But why should anyone care? Spare a thought for Martha Washington, who didn't even have a White House — it was being built. Bess Truman spent half her life at the family home in Missouri. Frankly, I'm surprised more of them didn't run away some good distance. There are probably reasons to criticise Melania Trump, but her having modelled nude, her refusal to live in the White House, or even her now oddly-immobile facial expressions, are not. The US would probably benefit from more nontraditional First Ladies, not to mention some female Presidents.

Traditionally, the First Lady has overseen all significant renovations at, and re-decorations of, the White House. Jackie Kennedy's makeover of the building generated immense public interest, and she famously took them on a tour of the place, in a great stroke of PR. But this task, as with many others, has sometimes become a loaded political matter, since the funds come from taxpayers. There was international outrage recently when Melania remodelled Jackie's Rose Garden. Yet Nancy Reagan spearheaded a truly epic White House-reimagining, including a set of china worth $200,000. At first, Melania seemed uninterested in the task, until Donald publicly said that he found the place to be *a dump*, whereupon she inexplicably became involved. So it goes.

Despite having no formal political power — whatever that means these days — and never receiving a pay cheque, the First Lady does have an Official Office, and a fairly good-sized staff, as mentioned before, although this fluctuates from one to the next.

Michelle Obama had 24 employees. Laura Bush had 18. Melania Trump has 15. And naturally, though unfairly, they make far less money than the Presidents. Well, of course they do. A woman's work is never done.

Yet amusingly, in the vast majority of cases, the First Lady has always recorded far higher approval ratings than her husband. One could argue, if one were mean-spirited (and notice that careful use of the American-subjunctive), that with a role limited to social and charitable functions, and let's-not-rock-but-rather-stabilise political causes, this is understandable. But it should not be so. Some First Ladies were hugely celebrated by the public, and are still today, long after their husbands, or at least their husbands' legacies, are all but forgotten. Eleanor Roosevelt is a legend today for her championing of human rights. Mary Todd Lincoln, Betty Ford ... the list goes on. The very words *First Lady*, to many millions, still instantly conjure up the figure of Jackie Kennedy, whose sheer style won over generations of women. When I think of Jackie, I always remember that after the shooting in Dallas, she refused to remove her blood-spattered coat, and wore it all the way back to Washington. It was, she said *so that they could see what they had done to him*. It is now preserved in the National Archives, away from any public view, until 2103. So I'll never get to see it, but you, dear reader, or your children, may well.

A quick postscript. Before any of these fabulous women, there was Julia Gardiner Tyler, the second wife of John Tyler, President from 1841 to 1862. The 10th, in fact. But who cares about him? Yet history remembers Julia, arguably the first celebrity FLOTUS. In her youth in 1839, she posed for an advertisement for a clothing emporium. Scandal. Her upper-class parents whisked her away to Europe for 'education'. Among her romantic dalliances were a German Baron, a Belgian Count, bachelor (and future President) James Buchanan, and (married) future President Millard Fillmore. Labelled in the press as *The Rose Of Long Island*, there were so many suitors her father had to rent extra lodgings to entertain them.

John Tyler first proposed to Gardiner at the White House Masquerade Ball in 1843, a mere five months after his previous wife had passed away. He was 30 years her senior, so for a full year, and to the delight of the press, she continually turned him down. After a series of odd events that included her father getting obliterated when a cannon misfired on the maiden voyage of the USS *Princeton* in 1844, and a brief dalliance with her future husband's son, John Jnr —what *is* it with these names? — she and the President eloped and married at the Church of the Ascension in New York. Only twelve guests attended and a press release was put out that the event was one of mourning Gardiner's father. To cut her wonderful story short, popular Polish dances were written about her, she rode round in a coach drawn by eight Arabian stallions, and was the first First Lady ever photographed, by the daguerrotype-pioneer Edward Anthony. I must stress — all this is but the merest taste. Her life was far more interesting than just these facts.

America could certainly do with more nontraditional First Ladies.

But, at least for now, Julia Gardiner Tyler's work is most certainly done. May she rest in peace.

* * * *

I will wager that almost none of you, dear readers, have heard of a place called Slab City. I certainly hadn't, when, during my — although I should say *our* (on which more later) — American tour in 2018, noticed an odd-shaped place on the Sat-Nav, about 190 miles south of LA. I asked *what on earth's that?* and our guide and driver Ramon replied *Miss Tresra, you do not want go there.*

Travelling with a lady with whom you are splitting up is ill-advised. But the tickets had been booked some months before and we both felt it a huge waste to squander an opportunity that many dream of: the proper US road trip. Neither of us were drivers, so we'd booked Ramon, and he was *in it to the end*, as they say on US road trips. Apparently. The trip was ostensibly to garner material for the book you are holding in your hands, but that was just an excuse for a proper US road trip, and it ended up becoming so much more. As US road trips are famous for doing. I'll attempt to tell it how it happened. A proper US road trip.

But what if I do *want to go there?* I asked Ramon.
Miss Tresra, then I say you are stoopid.
That I certainly am, I replied, *let's go.*

A word on us. The lady with whom I was travelling was a Czech lady with the face of an angel and a mind minted in the old Communist regime — nothing, absolutely *nothing* would intimidate her. Small teeth, blue makeup over the eyes. A glint of fading mischief. Me, dear reader, I hope you know by now. And Ramon was a person who took his job very seriously, and that was writ large across his face: *I just drive these fools.* Detached. His face often took on a reluctant smile, then an unreluctant one. Shoulders slung low, tiny feet. But he was companionable enough, and felt at ease with us.

Slab City, it turned out, was an abandoned military base. An abandoned military base that had developed and thrived. Well, perhaps *thrived* is wrong, since there was no access to running water, electricity or sewage-treatment. But it's residential, and that's how they like it.

They, the residents, call themselves Slabbers, and the State of California doesn't collect property taxes as there aren't any land-lords and it isn't an official town.

I ventured forth to talk with some of them. Ramon warned: *Miss Tresra, you will regret.* And the Czech tank added: *Don't worry Ramon, he* never *listens.*

So Miss Tresra walked around and talked to some Slabbers. It turned out that Slab City had become a bit of a tourist destination, albeit one of curiosity, and the locals had accordingly adapted and opened bars (from their bunkers or, more recently, trailers). Lots and lots of trailers. Really, lots of trailers. Founded in 1956, after the Marine Corps abandoned what they called Fort Dunlap, near the town of Niland (as with most things American, *near* is an elastic concept), Slabbers call it the Last Free Place in America. Fair enough.

There is no money in Slab City, rather one has to barter with what one has. So your humble author sang a song for a drink. The Slabbers seemed to approve, and showed me around. What did I sing? A little ditty from Act 1 of Puccini's *Manon Lescaut*.

'There's a system here,' explained Slabber Paul Holman — the third in line — 'you need skills in repair and construction at least. But now ...' he waved his arm vaguely, 'now they turn up like hippies. No skills. Nothing to bring. I used to work at Renaissance Faire, building sets. I knew what I was getting into. I was right cool.'

I resisted the temptation to make a few hippy jokes. I wasn't sure my humour would go down well around here, or indeed anywhere in America ...

Paul Holman the 3rd continued: 'It's normally 120 degrees in the summer, and the summer is long. And I mean long. Would you like another drink?'

'Yes please,' I said, 'it's hot even now.' It was nine at night. In late October. But the stars looked absolutely unbelievable, and the syllables were long.

'Sing us another song then,' he said, and I obliged. What did I sing for that second drink? Of course, the second aria from Act 1 of Puccini's *Manon Lescaut*, the go-to aria, I had always found, for awkward situations. High, but in an easy place in the voice, it usually worked. He continued:

'There's 4000 of us here. But some pussies go elsewhere during the summer. One summer we had only 600.'

I ventured: 'May I ask, but how did you get started?'

Holman the 3rd barely glanced at me before he continued: 'But you know that.'

'Yes, sorry, I meant ...'

'I know what you meant. You meant why am I here and what do I [pronounced aaaah] do to survive?' I must have nodded because he continued: 'We sell souvenirs at the outer slabs and we have a stage in the centre of town — the big ol' missile turret — and people come and put on performances there. We've had ...' he glanced down, as if recalling an ancestral indiscretion, '... the Rolling Stones, Mariah Carey ...'

'Sorry to interrupt, but are you sure they were the real Rolling Stones?'

He came back with the clincher. 'Who gives a shit? We live off-grid out here. If you say you can play — hey, you just sing. *You* just singed [sic] — who are we to judge?'

171

I found I quite admired his, and their determination. They weren't spouting conspiracy theories or hippy or Buddhist or Ram-Dam philosophies or celebrity-join-us claptrap. They just wanted to be left alone. So, after Paul offered me a last drink in exchange for the *Manon Lescaut* Act 3 aria, I asked:

'May I walk around a bit?'

'Of course, why ask?'

'To be honest, I'm British and I don't know if I might get shot...'

'Haha,' and it was a rich laugh, filled with stories of the hills and about an octave lower that your humble narrator's, 'you think we're all hillbillies.'

Before I could attempt to answer, he shoo-ed me off, into the town, cradling my drink in its flimsy biodegradable cup.

It was eerie, swaying between the big US turrets that were never used, except in exercise. Obsolete almost the minute they were built. Abandoned for a town of people to come and live how they want to, without outside interference. As I wandered, they handed me candles so that I wouldn't lose my way. Some offered food or lodging. I couldn't help thinking this was some sort of wonder-world, so long as one could live without the Internet.

And it was not windswept. Just a little dusty perhaps. And the lights were lit in all the little settlements of Slab City — all of them — and it made me think of school opening day, when all the children crowded through, some scared, others boisterous, still others half-hearted.

Then I knew. It would survive. I understood their reluctance to change. I understood why they occasionally got violent with outsiders who came in to try to change them.

It's primal.

It's love.

You never give up on your children.

I got back to the van around 5 a.m. Ramon had gone to sleep in the back, beside my Czech girlfriend, soon to be ex-. *Sweet*, I thought, and had a last cigarette out in that low California air. It's the kind of air you need to feel on your skin. It touches your fingers and it touches your toes. *That's why skin has always been the issue for Americans*, I thought, *not because they're a young country, or even*

172

because of sheer size, where sometimes your nearest neighbour can seem like a visitor from outer space. It's because of the skin.

I opened the door.

Miss Tresra. Welcome back.

Where the hell have you been?

I decided to have another cigarette.

* * * *

There's a room called the Anechoic Chamber. It's in South Minneapolis, Minnesota. If you had a cigarette in *there*, you'd beat yourself to death. It's the quietest place on earth. It has insulated walls of four-foot-thick concrete and double walls of insulated steel inside *them*, not to mention the three-foot-thick acoustic wedges that send sound back at you. A minute in there can apparently drive you insane.

Well, your humble author had been on the waiting list for five years. In 2019 he got the chance. Alas, not in the American one, but one in Nice, France. There are five anechoic chambers in the world — but Minneapolis was the first.

I managed a PB of 7.89 minutes. Personal Best.

Now, that that might strike you as inconsequential. But it wasn't. The best *ever managed* was 45.2, and the average is 2.2.

I can tell you some things about it. You have to remove all clothing — clothing *rustles* — you have to remove your glasses and contacts — you have to sit naked on a steel stool that doesn't move and is bolted to the floor. It is also one piece: no head bolted to the leg. And you instinctively close your eyes when the door *frishes* shut.

You sit there.

It seems like a dream of death, but a happy one. After a minute — or what feels like a minute — you start having visions. You feel your own blood flowing. No, you *hear* your own blood flowing. You want to cry. Or shout. You start to hear everything in your body, every tiny thing a body does. And you soon learn it does a lot. I scratched my foot and it sounded like an earthquake. It *felt* like an earthquake. And it was an earthquake — to my bodily system. I later learned that the total lack of reverberation sabotages your spatial awareness and causes loss of balance.

There are many accounts of people reporting feeling *ill* and *lost* and *disoriented* on the morning of September 11th 2001, before they had heard news of the planes hitting their targets. Scientists deduced that this was due to the fact that, as all aircraft had been grounded, people were unaccustomed to *not hearing stuff*. Obviously, UFO sightings went through the roof — and there were queues a mile long into Trauma Wards. Hell, it wasn't even a full moon.

I'm obviously not a superstitious man. You know that, if you've made it this far, dear reader, I hope. And hope is a good thing. But I do like surprises. Back there in the anechoic chamber I told myself to meditate. Breathe in and out, some kind of exercise all by itself. Inhale. Exhale. Tooooosh. Flooosh. I'm a singer, so I used my ribcage and diaphragm as I had been taught to. I calmed my brain. *Think of beautiful calm things.* The other side of my brain replied *You will die and be evil instantly.* I probably wasn't the best candidate for an anechoic chamber. I thought about dying, yes, the inevitable. And then suddenly birds, multi-coloured, filling your eyes with feathers, fuzzy ...

'Mr Williams? Mr *Williams?* Don't make me slap you again.'

'No, It's okay. No slap.' I woozed-to. Reality drew in. I said, '*That* has to be a record. I did it, no? Over an hour?'

'You were in there for almost eight minutes. We have your results here ...'

I was vaguely aware of him gesturing toward a machine that was busily printing out ... stuff. Scrolls and stuff. I expansively spread myself across the — very comfy — sofa, so thoughtfully placed in the come-to space. My body needed it. Ahhhhh, instantly this was good. Good stuff.

'You managed seven point nine eight minutes.'

He must have noticed my deflated expression, because he added: 'If it's any consolation, you did better than Anne-Sophie Mutter.'

'Thanks,' I said, pulling on my trousers, 'that's great.'

'Do you need anything?'

'Yes. To get as far away as possible..'

174

I understand, said the doctor, as he led me down the corridor ...

* * * *

Will be. Wait for. Want to. *Hoooooeeeeee.*

* * * *

I did toy with the idea, during these pages, of telling the sad story of Mary Mallon, or as she's remembered, Typhoid Mary: incarcerated against her will, and apparently unrepentant to the end.

But it felt a little uncomfortable given the situation at the time of writing.

The slim volume you hold in your hands was mostly put together during the 2020 Covid-19 Great Big Lockdown. We're in a second Lockdown as I write these words. (And a third lockdown as I add *these* ones, the final ones of the book, funnily, on New Year's Eve, at ten to midnight, during my final glance over the manuscript before I press Send.) There are many problems with these compulsory quarantines: difficulties of maintaining cloudless mental health, loneliness (although I was lucky enough to have Isolation Buddies), financial difficulties caused by being banned from working, and many more. But it did afford me an unbroken stretch of time — a rare luxury — to concentrate on this, *Fairytales and Oddities*. But this isn't the only thing I've been doing while confined to my preternaturally warm flat in Highgate.

We have entered the eighth month (November), and in that time, since March, I have filmed three full series of three different comedy shows (*Titbits With Williams* — from which this section of the book takes its name — *Kitchen Secrets With Williams*, which has proved a bit of a minor online hit — and *Morgenmuffel*, a mild horror/comedy hybrid), started a video diary (a *vlog* in street parlance) which has now passed the nine-hour mark, and recorded lots of songs and piano music from my living room. And it's all public, free to view, on YouTube, and it's all for you, dear Eli, my son. I also acquired many more things for your room (Fuzzy-Felt, a model MIG-29 fighter jet, the Usborne Puzzle Adventure books I had when I was young, a *Star Wars* chair ...) and for the flat in general (wall posters of *Apocalypse Now*, Tuesday Weld, *Once Upon A Time In America*, Peter Falk as *Columbo* ... 109 fridge magnets, yes, a little excessive ... a silver bathroom storage unit, a tortoise garden ornament, a full-length mirror ...) I also became the literal face of Coronavirus, in the book *Ezzy the Virus*, by my friend, the children's author (and scientist) Rachel Haywood. She, having naturally asked my permission, used a picture of me as a five-year-old — in fact possibly the first photograph of me in existence — there are no baby pictures as my troglodytic stepfather didn't allow them — and used it in her illustrations. So your daddy, to this and subsequent generations of kids, is what they'll see when they learn about how this particular Coronavirus worked and spread.

And I did lots of other things as well.

In this current climate we *all* feel like potential Typhoid Marys. We wear masks when we exit our homes. We practise "Social Distancing". The atmosphere is one of fear and distrust. Other humans, even our friends, look curious to us, unfamiliar and vaguely threatening: wild animals, pacing the cage. There is no sign of us musicians being allowed to return to work. Perhaps Mary Mallon *did* do it all deliberately, as she was so accused. After all, there were the name changes, the hair dyeing, the constant moving from place to place and family to family. By the end of her run she was estimated to have infected at least 51 people and caused three deaths. The words *super spreader* have been much on people's lips of late, and Mary was certainly one of them. She attempted to escape from hospital, was unlawfully imprisoned, had numerous medical tests performed on her body without her consent, and was ultimately banished to North Brother Island for the rest of her days. She died in 1938, and nine people attended her funeral at St Luke's Church, in the Bronx, less than two miles from where Julia Gardiner Tyler had married the President. My work in the US was done. I craved rain. I craved home.

* * * *

It started with a cigarette. As most stories do. Or, as a lot of stories do. Or ought to.

* * * *

One lights a cigarette. A scene is set. Was it Ibsen who said that if the audience sees a gun mounted above the fireplace in Act 1, that gun *has* to have been fired by Act 3? Or something like that. Anyway, one lights a cigarette. The glow is a tiny hum. This is important, because humans can't survive without such hums. Hums are what we rely on. Wait … what was that?

Some fly in my eye, no doubt.

* * * *

These titbits are entertaining, at least to me.

And Nigel. Oh, Nigel. Hats off to Nigel. *Jeeee*, as they say in Czech. May there be an afterlife, if just for him: a place where gannets are created equal, and given by scientists the chance to pursue happiness, unfettered by human interference.

But *this is* Act 3. And not Act 3 of *Manon Lescaut.* And that's no fly in my eye. What am I supposed to say before the curtain falls? What am I expected to say, my son?

There is a final story in this book that, I hope — and hope is a good thing — contains everything I have to say.

You, my son, my reader: you are all.

But who will fire the gun?

* * * *

And now the door closes, with a *frish*.

Alias Adora

A solid gaunt building, red and austere. At its base, five overflowing dustbins nestle together under a colonnade of arches not visible from the street. It appears at first inspection to be a stage-set, a regular prop, separated from each adjoining structure by dingy four-foot-wide alleys containing empty beer cans, crumpled Marlboro packets, discoloured condoms, broken glass, chipped teeth, dead leaves and the souls of men.

* * * *

At the top and bottom of the house the brickwork was chipped. It was marked, deeply. Big pieces kept flaking off. The façade sported eight windows, two on each floor, and the early September sunlight made each pane look gently slanted, opaque as limo-glass. Visitors often wondered, as they approached the front door through all the red dust, what the area had been like a couple of years before. Some must have noticed the rehabilitation of Redcliffe Gardens — Edwardian detached houses made over as cottages on the estate of Dracula's castle — and the invigorating advances of the Fulham Road. The PFI-funded space-age portico of the Kensington and Chelsea Hospital, bashful greasy-spoons, street-food cafés, pubs that seemed to have numbingly surrendered to the ratio of glamour versus injury. Of course, by 2012 and the advent of the London Olympics, in the average London street every other building had given up on civilian life and become an immigrant sweat-shop or brothel or church, yet at 28 Redcliffe Gardens an innocence remained, a patina of calm. And on the third floor of this dismal red block over yonder, Lenny Plinth was sweating into his bedsheets.

Despite being awake for some considerable time, he hadn't stirred. There was much to worry about. *How are things ever going to improve?* he thought. *Well, even if they don't, they can always get worse ...* Such thoughts.

Eventually he peeled himself off the sodden eiderdown and went into the bathroom. It was windowless and had recently been painted yellow. Cheerful; tasteless. In the toothpaste-spattered mirror Lenny regarded himself, coolly. Objectively. The yellow wasn't helping. His eyebrows were crusted as if his eyes had recently been glued shut. Neon murk beneath the sockets. Mouth a sticky salty cave, fluffed with dust, queasy with regret. He picked up a toothbrush and began scouring in there. It didn't go well. For a start, it hurt. Spots of weak blood in the sink. With a delicate shimmy, he sighed: *yes, it will only get worse from here.* Consider it a fabulous wrong. Such awful thoughts.

A Q-Tip withdrawn from the left nostril turned out to be richly bloodied, and Lenny regarded its scarlet bud with the detachment of the seriously ill. His hungover brain felt like millions of tiny maggots were trying to burrow their way out of it. Across his unresponsive brow eruptions bubbled.

He wasn't too worried. It was lifting.

Still, *things were bad.* Thoughts like these ...

* * * *

'Good lord, Milo, you might as well have just called it *Going To Pot*. And what's this about more money? What have you done with the money you received already?'

'Gone, innit. Need more. And you said book advances could be like written off for tax, or some such. Tax-*de*-or-*re*-duct. And what's wrong,' he added suspiciously, 'about my titles?'

Milo *The Maelstrom* Milkins was a famous snooker player. Perhaps more exactly, he was a famous snooker player who wasn't famous for playing snooker anymore. He was what TV dubs 'a personality'. Not quite a pundit: more an occasional celebrity-gameshow contestant or tabloidal Twitterer. It could also be argued that, by naming him Milo, Milo's parents had fallen at the first hurdle.

The man he was talking to was his agent, Frank Pullen, and Milo needed a second advance on his autobiography, having spent the first on messily divorcing his sixth wife, booze, gambling (usually cards — occasionally cock fights) and women. But never drugs — he considered drugs to be the preserve of *coloured folks*. With the

182

exception, obvs, of marijuana. This made sense to him, unlike much else. Some things are for *all* folks, not only some.

'I must say, while I think of you as a friend as well as a client, Milo, the original advance was five hundred thousand pounds. That's not just going to disappear from the publisher's memory ...'

Milo had been working on his autobiography for three years. He had so far produced only the title. In fact, that wasn't quite fair — he'd produced several titles, all of which had been delicately but firmly rejected by his publishers, Quex, Mutrix & Colas. Milo's titles had included *Travels with Cue, Cue & I*, the ampersand being a stroke of genius that came to him after beating up his ex-wife (Dawn) one sweaty Tuesday afternoon, the uncompromising *Screwing Cue*, the elegant — he was just happy to break the cycle — *Racking My Brain* and the peppy yet succinct *Cue And A With The Maelstrom*. This last one he conceived as an interactive memoir, with scannable QR codes in each chapter. He hadn't worked out what the QR codes would lead to, but that hardly mattered. Someone else could do all that ... Wait. A sudden impulse — what about leading to a games' page, where one could play — no, wait — *even better*, actually *bet money* on a game? More images swam into his brain, with £-signs attached. The logger-in could then indulge to his leisure. Only *his*? Well, yes. There weren't likely to be many female readers, let's face it. And Milo was a tad touchy about his titles for the simple reason that they seemed to be the only thing he could do when confronted by the blank page. Thoughts just wouldn't form one sentence followed by another. And he didn't appreciate the impotent feeling. Words didn't seem to be his *thing*.

He was a classic snooker winner — British, fulsomely racist, controllably alcoholic, hero to three generations of men from Yorkshire and above. By 'classic' player we should perhaps clarify our meaning. In this case we mean old-school in demeanour — mildly ravaged looks, an insolent way about the baize. And after controllably alcoholic, we should add: *just*.

'*Going To Pot* is good, but seems a little ... well, bollocks,' said Milo, without irony.

'Look, what have you got for me?' asked Frank Pullen. 'I could may be summon up some more money if you could send me some narrative.'

'What's narrative?'

'The book, Milo. The writing. The words within the book. Can you send me some of them?'

'Why didn't you just say so? I'll email it over now. The words, yeah? Not the pictures.'

'Thank God Milo, I await. Thank you. Do it now. Hang on ...' He drew breath. *What pictures?*'

'The pictures in the book. You didn't think it was all words did you? How dull. How bloody dull. No. All my favourite books have pictures in them, and I know my fans — their favourite books have pictures in them too. They will de*mand* pictures. I am a modern media beast. Trust. Sending now. It's all about pictures. Check the attachment. Cheers. Laters.'

With a moist sigh, Milo Milkins replaced the handset and gazed despondently across the garden. No one understood him. And the world was poorer for that, he felt. He understood victimhood.

He sorrowfully sparked a spliff and held the inhale.

* * * *

Lenny looked up his latest symptoms on Dr Google and diagnosed himself with Puffs lymph. Clearly that's what he suffered from:

> There are several reasons of the sore throat but some reasons are also considered as the main reasons like the germ which are the main cause of somewhat we understand and it is also right in the opinion of medical science that there a germ as well known as streptococcus this germ generally damage your throat and give you the irritation and the bad sore of the throat. Possibly there are other reasons like sinutitis diphtheria and measles leukemia that can be bad for your throat and give you more pain as you can think.

He thought: *This is so apt.*

> Whenever you go in the hospital then you would have seen that the people over there usually complaint about

the Puffed when they could have the problem like that their throat get dried and warm sometimes which is the result of the fever and chilling also which is the result of bad bacteria. Puffs lymph is the reason of the sore throat by which your throats get trapped into the bad pain. Sometimes if you could have felt that swallowing might be very painful and it is the total result of the sore throat which is the cause of the bad bacteria. If the exasperation of the throat reaches the air and it give you more pain as your throat get you in trouble. And it is also reason of the cold air when you are walking in cold season. One is the common reason as per my concern people must also be aware about it and that is the more cause of the bad throat can say the bad sore throat are the resultant of infection and the more bacterial action like if you have been using a toothbrush for a month.

Dr. T. Singh, FRCS, MRCS, FDSRCS, MFDS (RSC Eng)

I defo have puffs lymph, he thought.

Despite his psychosomatic sickliness, Lenny was a big guy — not tall, but compact. *Tight* was the word his ex-girlfriend had used, and she wasn't referring to his generosity on dates. There was solid musculature of the upper arms. Tight stretched skin over a road-map of veins. His mouth, when not animated, linked slow resentment to tepid petulance, and his eyes, a liquid innocent blue, held an element of contrition, as of a child on the verge of anticipated physical punishment, and hoping to avoid it by acting coyly. The late actor (and philanthropist and pasta-sauce magnate) Paul Newman once half-heartedly remarked that on his gravestone he wanted the inscription:

HERE LIES PAUL NEWMAN
WHO DIED A FAILURE
BECAUSE HIS EYES TURNED BROWN

Lenny's eyes were not quite Newman-blue, and smaller, and often seemed focussed on something irresistible (and invisible) one-foot in front of them. But they didn't make you uneasy. He simply hadn't learnt how to use them.

His clothes were perennially dowdy. A token T-shirt might read — DO LESS WORK: CAN'T BE ARSED. His tops were rock-star cast-offs that didn't hang well. They often looked like they had been put on wet and, when allowed to dry by body-heat alone, had done so in their own peculiar crinkled way. He looked like a guy who would enter a bookshop and reposition the Bibles and Qur'ans into the Fantasy section.

Hard brow, narrow chin, skeletal fingers. Lenny had also culti-vated a loping gait or hucksterish swagger that he liked to think created an impression on the un-inured. It didn't, but that hardly mattered. It boosted self-esteem, or some such nonsense. And Lenny needed all the nonsense, especially self-esteem. Such boosts reminded him, daily, indeed every minute, that he was the only black man in the building, never mind the street. And don't get him started on Fulham.

That morning he was wearing a grey T-shirt that had been cut into a vest-top. Strictly speaking, it wasn't that day's choice — he'd woken up in it. And the cut-off look was stylish. Frayed strands on the shoulders that looked curiously like epaulettes. Lenny opened the window and let in some meaty London air. Sucked on it and rolled it around his mouth like expensive cigar smoke.

After checking emails, he selected a pair of tiny binoculars from the solitary white bookcase — mostly given over to video games — and raised them to window/shoulder level. Grinning, he imag-ined himself as a Superman/Everyman crossbreed, gazing over the city from some clandestine garret. Or was that Batman? No matter. He searched for the girl opposite.

She'd moved in only recently, but Lenny was smitten. With all the helplessness that that entailed. He was surprisingly shy around women, despite his appearance. The old self-esteem problem again. Because he'd been out of work for a long while, he felt useless to women, and uselessness is a sure impotence-inducer in men like Lenny Plinth. Being part of the game mattered. Useful-ness was everything. Not that he was physically impotent, only psychologically so. He also imbibed a good deal of alcohol, and while he didn't consider himself an alcoholic by any means, he was a tad touchy about the amounts he consumed. Last night for example — don't get him *started*.

* * * *

Exactly six minutes later, Frank Pullen called back. For a brief while Milo couldn't make out a word he was saying, because it sounded as if Frank Pullen was choking to death.

'So you like it?' asked Milo, evenly.

After another few minutes, Milo made out, '... this is very contentious stuff. And it's not about what you're properly famous for. An autobiography is supposed to be about your career, not your views about ... well, *black people*.'

'What's contentious mean? Use words I know ...'

'Yes, and the homophobia and the ... Oh, *Christ*. Think of the pub*licity* Milo.' There was a pause. 'The *press*.'

Milo yawned expansively and said, 'Say no more. It's fine. The press loves me.'

'They'll destroy you.'

'No chance. They love me. Bloody adore me. I'm Britain, me. *Admired*.' Blood rose a little in his neck. 'Destroy me, lol, *me*? Like on the table? No chance. I'm not even playing till next month, and that's only against *Timetable* Timmy. Seniors, ain't it?'

'Milo, please listen to me ...'

'Dude, worry not. You of no faith. You wouldn't know ...'

But Frank Pullen did know. He knew all too well. The final years of *The Maelstrom*'s professional snooker career had been pock-marked by well-publicised outbursts. The time Milo head-butted the only black player on the tour — a sepulchral Muslim with a refulgent beard, whom Milo accused of leaving tiny wiry hairs on the table, post-shot, to disrupt his play. The time he was sent off for mooning a visiting business delegate of potential African sponsors. The time he outraged women's groups by holding his cue in front of his trousers and miming athletic sexual action two-feet behind a female referee ... It wasn't pretty. None of it was pretty. Milo was still sore about that last one. He claimed a set-up. If *female groups* had *infiltrated* the match, he argued, then they simply had it coming. They *couldn't have been there for the game.* Obvs.

Incredibly, none of these misadventures seemed to dent his fanbase, which, if one could reasonably gauge by what one read in the press and online, was louder and stronger than ever, now that he was no longer winning matches on a regular basis. It should be noted, however, that Milo was a legend on the circuit. Despite having won only three ranking titles during a twenty-year career, *The Maelstrom* was twelve times a World Championship semi-finalist, and fifteen times a Masters semi-finalist. More than once he had had a wonderful and inspiriting fight-back from many frames down, and had delivered his share of incredible shots — five YouTubed-massés, crawls, drags, run-throughs, deep screws, reverse-doubles, double-kisses, jumps, swerves, stuns, controlled cannons, controlled safeties, rescued backspins, piqués, pushes, plants, checked-side, caroms, plain-ball runs … Hell, for a while, even his miscues were news. His matches had often gone on well into the wee small hours of British TV, and perhaps this was part of the appeal: if enough people watched you being brilliant while they got drunk, anyone could become a hero.

'Listen to me …'

But Milo was enthused and not to be stopped. He said, 'Been through all that. Bad press is good press, innit?'

'That's not exactly the saying, no. And that's not how it works …'

'Frank. Worry not,' pronounced Milo, luxuriously. 'It's all good. Water off my back. Ducks, like. Just publish the stuff. Get it out. Into the world. The world needs to see me. *Read* me. Understand me. And my story, obvs. With pictures. What're the probs?'

'Right now I just need a little bit of actual unbiased writing. Narrative, sorry, words, to keep the sponsors keen. Without bigotry. There's a lot riding on this. Please lay off the booze today and write some … some … text … okay, *words*. Can you do that? Please? With no racism or hatred of anyone?'

Whatever.

Milo sat down, no, *hunkered* down with his laptop in a kitchen armchair. Bring on *writing*, he thought. I can do this crap with words. I'll show them all.

* * * *

He had seen her for the first time two weeks ago. The roofs had been oddly blanketed by sparrows. A smell of salami in the almost-warm air. Through reviving trees, across the street, four Ron Jeremy lookalikes were moving possessions into the house. It looked like company policy — identical moustaches and paunch-stretched logo-ed blue T-shirts with white golfing caps. The branding on the side of their long yellow lorry read: WE'RE TRANSPERTS. Half-heartedly, Lenny selected a pair of mini-binoculars (almost opera glasses) to see who was moving in. Then she appeared from behind a packing crate.

He felt physically touched, as if someone had pushed him against a wall. Not winded, but astounded. A great mechanical B-movie monster gone haywire. All legs, legs unfolding in inadequate space. Then he felt ... peace. Unfamiliar, but recognisably good.

Barefoot, and delicately bouncing like a ballerina, she instructed the Ron Jeremys — that one there, yes — to position things. Lenny felt her proximity to them to be morally wrong. Just, there. Yes. She was wearing Dr Martens boots with purple tights. Travelling up, Lenny discovered an off-white midriff-top and a huge mustard scarf. He'd never seen anyone so beautiful. She had cautious eyes and a face that had he not seen it for himself, he would have invented it in his imagination.

Lenny inhaled ... Hsssss. Tossing that nut-brown hair, but only to see how it behaved when provoked, there was a curious colour about her. As of someone who'd spent a month in a sleeping bag. A glass ashtray flashed tiny angry triangles onto her face.

Lenny exhaled ... Tsssss. He could barely breathe. Smiling at the memory. From the first sighting he'd watched her for a few minutes each day and become more besotted. Every night in bed, as he lay there waiting for sleep, he'd meet her. It had always been that way — sleep bored him. He had to think of pleasurable things to bring it on. Being next to her was the most pleasurable thing he could imagine, a chaste, almost teenage love. But Lenny was thirty-three, and these things seldom cross boundaries well.

Happily, a week later, he'd met her twice. She'd been entirely civil the first time, if a little distant. But given what he'd been imagining, how could she not seem so? He recognised this. The first time was when he took over some mail. His house was 28, her's 33, diagonally opposite, a tad to the left.

On sloppily printed or smudged letters, the 8 and the 3 could resemble one another. Lenny found himself to be deliriously thankful of this quirk when, one morning, he found a magazine addressed to her in the communal hallway of his building. Unfortunately, it didn't bear a name, just Occupier, but he girdled himself to take it over and buzz. A coldish day. He introduced himself as a neighbour who'd seen her moving in, wanted to welcome her to the 'hood, and just wanted to *drop this off.* Up close, she was even more enchanting. Full, unabashed shoulders, eyes full of human need, but with a taint — as if the world around were some private fabrication. But no dismay. It was a powerful gaze, one not out of place in the films he never watched anymore. Films in which carriages changed colour and people were called Judy and Matlida and Lawrence, and animals held conversations. He was smitten all right.

She thanked him. Other things on the mind. A movie on the TV, emails to reply to, perhaps. That night, when he picked up the binoculars (newly purchased for this purpose), she was pottering about the flat, putting up pictures. Having a glass of white wine. Annoyingly, he couldn't tell what the pictures were of.

The second time had gone much better, it seemed to him. Meeting on the street by accident — although not by accident at all, as Lenny had plunged down the stairs when he saw her leave — they joked about locals bars ... She wasn't sure which was the best ... he made a flippant remark about a particular one being a front for the BNP or EDL or generic Nazis, and how another one on the Fulham Road was superior, in every sense ... They chatted for ten minutes. About how London was ever-changing, about the mail-confusion, about the area and local establishments ... She was called Abra, although apparently everyone called her Adora ... She was a journalist ... And then it happened. She suggested a drinks evening with friends, as no one "does housewarming parties anymore". He almost fainted. A time was set for the following Wednesday, at 7 p.m. He realised he'd walked her to the tube station and waved her off. New, unfamiliar things.

That night he felt an intimation of *fitting in*. Whatever that meant, to *white folks*.

* * * *

Milo Milkins looked like a guy you could enjoy a pint with (the litmus test of British popularity): not too perfectly shaven, public face affable, without excessive creepiness. Importantly, the fault lines of personality were not writ large. One hundred and seventy-eight centimetres high, with a hollow body of dark tempo-slowing places, he was shorter than what was currently fashionable among the best players, and had subsequently suffered, dropping out of the Top 16 List mere days before his thirty-fourth birthday,

His style wasn't radically different from them ... only perhaps the grip, which 'curled out' from the pinkie during run-throughs, and for which the commentators made jokes about his upbringing. (Apparently only the poor kids did this. No one quite knew why. It was one of the mysteries of the baize. One theory had it that cheaper cues were more prone to splintering around the grip, hence lower-class kids knew to withdraw the skin quicker. This was mere speculation, naturally, although ...)

In the balmy late 90s, Milo blazed a trail through the sport, with advertising endorsements for acne-cream, non-alcoholic beer, a brand of cough-relief (oral only — despite his 'people's' urging, Milo wouldn't countenance the other kind) and running gear. By 2012 it was online dating, bingo and poker. An avatar in his likeness jerked and joked onscreen, juggling betting chips. He appeared to have it all. But, behind the scenes, a faltering occurred.

Chrysanthemum, his 4th wife, had an affair with a black guy named something like Mike, or Trike, or Crikey — she was never sure on that. Milo forgave her. He figured that, given forgiveness, she'd have to marry him and be faithful evermore: a delectable trope. Except, she didn't comply. She left. A *bolter*, Milo decided. He festered and began to see foulness everywhere. The TV suddenly seemed full of stabbers, all black, to his mind, and all coming to get him. Driving — or rather being driven — through central London late at night, he'd glimpse a lean and hooded figure folded over a form in an alley. But, since he'd los*t the run of the balls* and was losing almost every match he played, for Milo, it was all about *him* and *them*.

Boy, was Milo in Blacktown. He saw it on Reality TV shows everyday. *They*, black people, were there for entertainment: okay. Almost exclusively monochrome, as was the prison system in America (it seemed to him: *just lock them all up*), Reality TV helped him through the day. He saw it everywhere. He slowly stopped being able to see beyond the subject.

During this time he began to see only blacks in dreams, black balls that is, all of them un-potable. 7 after 7 after 7 getting away from him — at best rattling the jaws, at worst rolling silently (with no plosive cue-ball connection) to the end cushion. Where there used to be rich clusters of reds shattering everywhere and nudging the blue or pink to just over a corner, there were now only popping, hollow blacks. He never told anyone about this, but privately, he became resigned to his talent withering away.

But then, things were looking up. Milo had been *writing*...

* * * *

'*Who's* the girl of the 21st century? *Who* gives up the Pill? *Who* takes sex to outer space? Who almost dies of *pleasure?*'

Lenny held his head as the band began their set, and smiled with every kind of inauthentic feeling: a crease here, a wobbling tear there.

He had put off the desirable prospect of more sleep to join his downstairs neighbour Greg in The Hurricane Room — pool, snooker, darts, drinks. He felt he ought. Greg was new, too: he'd arrived a mere week before Adora. But Lenny had known Greg before: had indeed recommended the flat below to him, when Greg had had a regrettable run-in with his old landlord over a habit of thowing carrier bags full of empty beer cans into the disused back garden. A recommendation he found himself virulently regretting.

The live band was called *Firmaments Four*, a microscopically talented, yet preposterously attractive girl group. Every song was in E-flat major. It gave their set a certain hypnotic quality, but it hadn't helped his and Greg's pool game. Lenny lost the match 8 – 2 (best-of-15), and they were now at a corner table, several empties between them. Greg was in the middle of a horrible speech:

'... such fetching freckles. She's a little honey, man. *Dude* — look at that hair. Let that hair down, she'd be burned as a witch. L-o-l.' He actually said it — l, o, l, not laugh-out-loud. Lenny felt his brain involuntarily constrict. The abbreviation had as many syllables as the full phrase. Hatred was only natural. Greg continued: 'And those hot pants. With a midriff top. *Quality*. Peppery though. Looks like it. A handful. Give her a month and she'll have a gym in your basement.'

Greg was talking about the lead singer of *Firmaments Four*, who was still screaming at the back of the bar. Like ordinary people, lunchtime drinking was making Greg lairy. Lenny had always privately considered this word to be a combination of loquacious and hairy. Perhaps the etymology was sound. Who knew? Still, afternoon drinking didn't affect him that way, he was used to it, and the mood had darkened. Tired of playing along.

'So, Abra. How did you two meet?'

Greg flashed a set of powerful Hollywood gnashers that made Lenny self-conscious and momentarily dizzy.

'Well, funny you should ask. I just like got talking to her. Like we hit it off. She's hot, no?'

Lenny shrugged. Inwardly pooped, outwardly ...

'*Look at you*,' laughed Greg, 'you know she is. Eight three and she's some burn-up totty. What a day. Didn't know *you* knew her. Eight three. God. What happened to you? She mentioned you yesterday, like, first time.'

'Two. Eight *two*. She mentioned me. Yes?'

'Yeah, Eight two, right. Like, even worse. I'm thinking of asking her out, actually. Like, at some point.'

'Yes?'

'Indeedy-doo-da.' They clinked glasses and drank. '*Say* ...' This was phrased like a statement, not a question. Lenny didn't say anything or even look up. He felt mortally tired, in the bones, in the spirit, in the skull.

'Yes?'

'We're all going out on like Friday. Like, why don't you come?'

Lenny acquiesced. As they got up to leave, the lead singer of *Firmaments Four* launched herself off the tiny stage and began attacking a dilapidated group of men. It seemed one of them had thrown something at her, mid-song, a dart or pork pie.

On the street, sunlight blinded. It was physically uncomfortable, but only for a moment. Like stepping on to a stationary escalator, or emerging from a morning cinema jaunt. Above, jet trails formed Xs in the sky. Kisses on a long overdue godly postcard to the planet.

Cluttered foliage.

Greg staggered off back to his job in the city.

Lenny staggered home and slept for sixteen hours.

He had dreams about staggering and about having never been born.

* * * *

'So what precautions are you taking for Hurricane Philbert?' asked Frank Pullen. 'It's going to hit you know. You're right in the path.'

'I'm not in the bath, I haven't had a bath for three weeks ....'

'No, the *path*, Milo. Of the hurricane.'

'Yeah, all good. Er ... What's the hurricane?'

'*Milo* ... Jesus. Are you joking me? No? Strong winds and flooding for your part of Britain ...'

'What do you mean, *my* part? It's *all* mine. I *am* Britain. Remember the 1991 final? Yeah? I was eighteen nil down, couldn't be *worse* against *Timetable* Timmy – consistently consistent, but what did I do? I *rallied*. I came back out roaring. Cueing for Britain. A bulldog. That's who *I* am ...'

'Yes, sorry Milo, and thank you. But Hurricane Philbert will be bad. Please prepare.'

'But what did *he* do? Philbert?'

'No, it's not about that, they just name storms boy girl boy girl. This one's a boy and it's coming your way …'

Milo sucked in some expensive cigar smoke and narrowed his eyes. 'What do I have to worry about *here*?'

Here was Milo's vast mansion. It was modelled on Tony Montana's final big white mansion in *Scarface*, a film he loved for many reasons — the quotability, the luridness, the girls … Most of all he loved it because of the unfair sting followed by mild mirth he felt whenever he heard it had been *adopted by the black community* or was the film that '*best spoke to the African-American sensibility*'. The unfair sting — which always came first — was pain that so many of the people he loathed could love the same thing he did. It was also a sense of unfairness that this had somehow wronged the film about which he felt so protective, and his fatherly defences flared. Secondly, the delicious aftertaste, mild mirth — this was a flood of gladness that of *course* it was loved by African-Americans — there were drugs, guns and amorality galore, and hardly any blacks. And Milo felt very strongly that if there's one thing blacks hate more than anything else, it's other blacks.

In the film, the house is Miami-palatial, CCTV-ed, high-walled and gated … Not that these things did Tony Montana any good when Alejandro Sosa's henchmen came for him. It was fronted by six pillars and four pools in the segments of a square, divided by footpaths, a fountain at the centre. Milo's recreation wasn't so cinematic. He didn't have *that* much money, but it was an adequate approximation.

'Just *consider* getting to higher ground,' said Frank Pullen. 'At least do that.'

'Will do,' said Milo, as he tossed the handset onto the fag-burn-pocked sofa. Then, to no one: 'I'm off to the pub.'

The local pub, *The Jugged Rabbit*, was a half-mile-away downhill, at the bottom of a valley. Milo took the Snowhammer, a vehicle so badly designed for such crappy British terrain that it barely merited mention. Suffice to say, he walked most of the distance. Once in, and drinks served, a young lady moved nearer to the bar and ordered a white wine while still nursing her last.

Within the hour, everyone present realised that they weren't getting out. The water that had started to seep, then slosh, then glug under the doors, greeted by 'Come on!', and 'Give it your best,' seemed, inexorably, to *just keep on going*. Milo, spirit of Britain, knew what he had to do. He clambered onto a table — and the young woman's hand went to her pocket — and began a song. 'Come on,' he shouted. 'How's this one, my little friend?

Little Miss Muffet wanked on a tuffet
With a dildo the size of her arm ...
Along came a n*****
Whose cock was much bigger
And did her some permanent harrrrrrrmmmmm.'

And thus it continued until 3 a.m. *Need for leave*, thought Milo, vaguely. *I need to go* ... He did need to go, but not to the toilet. Time was crushing him.

Wobblingly, he waded out. The girl clicked the button *off*, and decided how she was going to make it through the night herself.

* * * *

Lenny Plinth had been many things in his thirty-three years on this planet called Earth ... Toy-seller, publisher's assistant, courier switchboard-operator, snooker-table sweeper, electricity meter reader, handheld computer-operator for London Buses, a cleaner at a garden centre. There was nothing that held his attention for long. He hated himself much of the time. What was life about? What was it all for?

One of the odd things that love did was make you want to be richer. Unfortunately, it didn't make you less lazy or more motivated. Lenny didn't doubt for a second that he was in love. In his dreams he and Abra, no, Adora, broke the glass under the canopy. He was Jewish in his sleep.

Careful not to jolt his head too starkly, Lenny made the kitchen and started the kettle. Mornings were alien. The enemy. Time felt dangerous, any action capable of being one's last. That's what love does to you, he thought. It warps. A tiny movement — oh, *no*, stay still.

The kettle finished boiling with a satisfied gurgle. He flicked the radio app on. *Mass flooding through the areas of* … He flicked it off again and poured boiling water over chocolate powder. Warm damp towel smell. After a microwave-heated burger — cold in the centre — he decided to scale the difficulties of the bathroom.

The mirror was the worst. It gave: a grave man with a quiet voice and carefully formed opinions. Standing very still, it was believable. But why should it be so? The sense of other people alive in the building all around him. After the strange slumber of medication; that spooky collective sleep, where colour didn't matter. Colour subtracted. He no longer dreamed in colour — it was *all* black and white. Someone had told him that this was to do with malnutrition, or malnourishment or some such. Who knew? Testing your feelings on yourself before others.

Mirror. His beard had gone crazy. Lenny briefly considered if he'd slept for *two* nights, not one. A Krakatoa of facial hair in five hours? Deciding he needed a new diagnosis, Lenny consulted Dr Google again:

> If anybody is reading this article and who is suffering from diarrhoea they do not worry and be careful and we are going to give some special tips which can be good in the diarrhoea and they can be very good to use it and this is been quite easy whenever you are going to use it. And this is good to use in the nearly future when you get trapped by the diarrhoea. The very first thing is that you must be ready when you have it and need to wrath of it. There are several possible reason why people going to have this big reason and that is the whenever you are having the dirty water in your bathroom then you need to clean out this water or you can dash some types of the medicine provided by the government and basically suggested by the doctor …

Puffs lymphs he could live with. That was better. You could touch that.

Adora wasn't home, so Lenny went to the pub. As he left Redcliffe Gardens, the clouds looked whisked, helicopter-scoped.

Welcome to the mental-health hotline. If you are obsessive-compulsive, press 1. If you are co-dependent ask someone to press 2 on your behalf. If you suffer from multiple personalities, press 3, 4, 5 and 6. If you suffer from paranoia, just hold and we're tracing your call. If you are delusional, press 9875643 and your call will be transferred to the Mothership.

He glanced at his phone. No calls.

Typical. You couldn't win.

* * * *

Milo Milkins found himself holding against a force of water he'd never believed possible. His heart felt limp and nasty. The landlord of *The Jugged Rabbit* had corralled everyone upstairs and allocated sleeping quarters, but Milo, pride of Britain ... Look at him wade out — look at ...

Milo wasn't sure what was happening at all. He had drunk far too much and was trying to keep his shit together. A *rage* seemed to be going on around him. A car went past. Then a boat went past. Wait ... *floated* past. Then he heard it, the thin tiny cry for help.

Milo looked. Over the rolling rapids a little boy was clinging to a lamppost. *Fuck.*

Milo set out, batting away obstacles, clearing the eyes, sober now, suddenly.

Unbidden, thoughts of pinks rushed in. Missed pinks. The World Championship he'd won when, putting too much top-spin to come back off the cushion to reach a red on the side, the pink jumped on the rail and ran, trickling in the opposite pocket for a four point advantage and leaving his opponent needing two snookers. All pinks, all pinks. Until only the black remained, balls against the swell.

The little boy was in a shop doorway, holding on to a — what *was* that? A car bonnet speared by a tree. It was all about to go. Milo grabbed him and held fast to the doorframe. It was the only way. It was ...

Those still in *The Jugged Rabbit*, including the girl with the camera, saw Milo grab the boy and save him.

Well.

Well. Things could certainly be said to have picked up for Milo after Tropical Storm Philbert hit the south of Britain. The police dinghy volunteers in HiViz vests who'd rescued him and the kid (mute and trembling like a tiny woodland creature) and the paramedics who'd treated them on higher ground — minor injuries for Milo and the kid ... okay, Milo suffered cuts and bruises. The kid had mild hypothermia, chipped teeth, a broken arm, two toes and a cheekbone, and complications after swallowing contaminated water — spoke to journalists at the hospital. They described Milo as 'A true sporting hero', 'selflessly himself', 'a born man', 'a true man, greater than any of his performances on the baize' and 'a bloke who deserves a knighthood if anyone ever did'.

He was duly presented with the Sports Personality Of The Year award a month later by the BBC, the first time a sportsperson no longer active in their field of competition had been accorded the privilege. It was front-page news not only in Britain, but in Scotland and Ireland too. Wales had never dug Milo much. The red top bloids proclaimed him Man Of The Year, and one of them raised money to produce a limited-edition beer-mat to commemorate his actions. This was only partly successful, due to the unfortunate print design that caused the two angels perched on Milo's shoulders to somewhat resemble golliwogs. Still, the mats became collectors' items and still sell for huge sums on eBay to this day.

Magazines quarrelled to photograph him in his snugglies by swimming pools, sipping ridiculous drinks with tiny umbrellas in them. It helped that he came across as self-deprecating. In fact, it was just stupidity, but the press often confuse the two ...

When he accepted the SPOTY award, the interviewer, a stalwart of respectable journalism asked:

'So, Milo Milkins. *The Maelstrom.* Literally. Yes! YES!!! Man of the hour, a rescuer of children — who are here tonight to applaud you, by the way, with their grateful mother ...'

I applaud, indeed love, *the plural use of children*, thought Frank Pullen, backstage. *One kid great, two kids always better.*

Suddenly there was a lingering close-up of the mother on a

huge screen for the studio audience, but not hidden from Milo's peripheral vision. He thought he was going to pass out, but …

'Give them a big hand, everyone …'

Yeah, but …

'Genius of the green baize, GENIUS, television wit …'

'Could we get on with it …' Milo badly needed a drink, and also a piss. TV is all about waiting around to hit your mark, say your bit, flash your most insincere smile, and he hadn't had any booze in almost twenty minutes. He also hadn't had an opportunity to use the toilet in over an hour. Both impulses were now urgent.

'In*cred*ible. How humble you are. HUMBLE, ladies and gentlemen!!! How unable to face your own inescapable hu*man*ity …'

Huge applause. Milo uncrossed and then recrossed his legs for the seventh time. 'Look,' he said, 'I don't know what you're on about, I mean, what you're talking about. Obvs.'

'How utterly amazing, ladies and gentleman, he pretends not to know what he is. AMAZING!!! So Milo, we must ask …'

Milo's eyebrows went up and down. The presenter did an über-pause.

'… what was going through your mind during those terrible forty minutes? Those forty minutes when it was just you and Dantrell? The boy you saved …'

Milo flinched. Incredibly, he realised that he'd never actually heard, or at least not taken in, the kid's name before.

'Well,' he replied, his bladder now a cannonball threatening to burst his cummerbund, 'I and Dan … Dantrey and me … I mean, Tandan, we was just waiting, innit? Waiting. Waited. Yeah, whatev, obvs. Wasn't we?' Milo looked around desperately. Anything to be somewhere else: a toilet, a toilet, this award for a toilet.

'Wow. Just … *wow*. LADIES AND GENTLEMEN: WOW!!!'

This time the clapping went on for a very long time. Milo almost glanced at his new IWG 1999, but remembered that Frank had told him not to. Instead he looked around quizzically. Little boy. Smile, wave, nod. All good. Anything, just anything to keep his mind off his nuclear bladder, lovely warm piss and beautiful beer … Ah, thoughts like these …

Sometime later, and with alarm, he noticed the audience was still clapping. Then the host picked up again, tears running down both cheeks. She said: 'Your old nickname *The Maelstrom* seems more appropriate than ever, since your courageous actions. How do you feel about this? How do you FEEL?'

'Listen,' said Milo, shuffling frenziedly. 'Well, yeah, there is that.' His mouth flexed, deeply. 'That, and I just want to say: "I love you all", and I need to go. Now. I should go.'

'Incredible. INCREDIBLE! Isn't he totally incredible?' The audience went insane, whooping and braying. Milo literally needed *to go*, but hey ho. 'One last question: Milo *The Incredible Maelstrom* Milkins, how did you feel when you rescued that adorable little black boy?'

'It's not about the colour of his skin,' intoned Milo, 'but rather the content of his character.' His belt behind the cummerbund had become a serious obstruction by this point, and he shuffled from side to side, in urinary agony, as the crowd went supernova. His interviewer, herself a TV legend, said:

'Milo. You are some kind of a man. SOME KIND OF A MAN LADIES AND GENTLEMEN!!!'

Who else could welcome in the new? Decorum must be observed.

Backstage, Milo made the toilet and pissed for a full 70 seconds.

* * * *

'Yes, I have it.'

'*Really*?' said Frank Pullen. 'Let me hear it then.'

Abra played the recording. There was silence, while next moves were considered. The day was a rich mineral blue. Frank Pullen finally said: 'Let's say that's real …'

'It *is* real. I was there …'

'Right. It's real. For you. Christ, come on, don't insult your own intelligence. Or mine. Audio can easily be faked. No one's going to believe this. Milo Milkins is a National Treasure. He's …'

'There's more.'

Frank Pullen fanned his fingers out behind his ears. After some terse seconds he said: 'Okay. What? Don't fuck with me. If there's more, give it up.'

'There's video.'

'Jesus,' said Frank Pullen. '*Jesus.*'

* * * *

Milo Milkins was nursing a glass of £55-a-bottle white, a drink in the upper echelons of his standard alcohol outlay, and strictly reserved for emotionally difficult occasions. Tiny rivulets were stuttering down the glass, measuring time. That morning's paper was beside him on the sofa. It was opened to the Entertainment section. Beneath the headline *Placido Domingo Announces Thirteenth Final Retirement* was a NIB (News In Brief) that read:

Is Britain's current favourite sportsman Milo "The Incredible Maelstrom" Milkins soon to be exposed as a closet racist? We hope not, but a journalist claims to have video evidence that this is the case. We await further information.

Milo took a swig of the Joseph Drouhin Puligny-Montrachet and felt momentarily gladdened. A positive sensation: the first he'd had since that morning's awful phonecall from Frank. But then sourness reappeared. His SPOTY award was on the sofa too, half covered by the newspaper, and he scuffed at it with a nail. Sourness everywhere. Was this what clinical depression felt like? Personality snivelling and coy, everyday things making you ill?

Of course he couldn't consciously recall any public racist outbursts, but then he had been some sips deep at the time the journalist claimed to have filmed him in *The Jugged Rabbit*, mere moments before his heroic rescue of the boy, little drowning Danson. No, wait, Danell? Dantoine? *Dammit.* And he hadn't only been imbibing one liquid: blame *that*, he thought, with a misunderstood flinch, if you don't like my personality. *I'm the true victim here.*

What was this all about? It seemed inconsequential. To Milo, racism was as natural as breathing. He believed in different species of human, just as he did in different species of animal. Someone had privately once commented, at some celeb bash or other, that only racists think racism is natural, but Milo couldn't grasp that: too big a leap. When Milo was born, back in the Cadillac-fin days and Miami-bright 1970s, racism used to signify disapproval on a genetic level – the sting of absolute hatred, without sense. It meant something. Now, that wasn't the case. Now the term semed dilapidated and resigned. It was now *racist* to comment on a haircut, or titter at a cultural quirk. The world was regressing. *Racism* certainly appeared to have rattled its clack. That was justification enough, thought Milo, to cut him some serious slack. Ah, the poetry of my utterly misunderstood existence. He sighed and took another swig.

We see him there, on the sofa — snooker redacted — utter belief in no talent. The movement of wine to lips, that space casting a shadow on the TV screen: cinematic — but artifice with no art. Yet we root for him, do we not?

Suddenly full of vim, Milo redialled Frank.

As he listened to Frank talking, complex expressions worked their untidy way across his face. Braving the dragon's breath, and watched by the afternoon sun, as wide as a dinner plate — naughty, naughty. The whole world globed in a wine glass. Something was forming in his brain, jerking along like crackling old war-footage newsreels. Frank Pullen had said the journalist's name. *Abra Greco*.

In Milo's mind, all he had to do was find Abra Greco, and force her to not publish the story. Details were fuzzy. But it would all work out fine and dandy. Whistling a carefree tune. Now that the floodwaters had receded, the trees outside were fully alive, leaning on their elbows, watching through his patio doors.

Feeling primal in the limousine later that night, on his way to *The Jugged Rabbit*, Milo called an old girlfriend, who was now a policewoman, and a stalwart supporter of his. In his phone she was listed as M Hirsch Cop. He asked for the journalist's address. WPC Melania Hirsch obliged.

Outside the car, London quivered like a paper lantern. Things were going to get better. Milo had hope. And hope was a good thing.

'Hey,' said Milo, to his driver, Nigel, 'forget what I said. Forget the pub. I want to go into town. Fulham. I need to check something.'

Milo had never once, in all his driver's employment, changed his mind about a visit to *The Jugged Rabbit*, so this had to be something important, or at least pressing. The car slowed and idly lurched to the right.

* * * *

Lenny Plinth couldn't remember a more decrepit and miserable morning. Yet this was ... different. Life was touching his fingers and life was touching his toes. The world had never looked so beautiful, as, barely a fortnight since the widespread flooding across the south and south-west of Britain, a sudden gout of snow had blown in off the harsh North Sea. To Lenny, watching the children below throwing snowballs, it all looked sepulchral, cadaverous, even. He smoked cigarette after cigarette and flicked the butts down onto the front steps: fizz, fizz, fizz. Occasionally, light from some passing truck threw a beam across the row of jars on his kitchen windowsill (growing basil and chives), and cast a leaning shadow on the wall to his left. It was the exact distance between his lips and cigarette. Lenny often thought the seasons should be reconfigured. Christmas should begin in March; summer should last until at least October. A three-month shift would bring the weather back in line with traditional expectations.

Lenny's troubles had begun in earnest the moment Greg told him in the Hurricane Room (two weeks earlier) that he intended to ask Abra out. A lifelong snooker and pool fan, Lenny hated losing games, but not as much as hearing Greg — whom he privately thought of as a dull token City Guy — express his alarming interest in the girl he dreamed of every night and thought of the moment he awoke. My sun rises and sets with her, he thought, savouring the whimsical, silly cinematic cliché. He knew he was Greg's token Black Friend — everyone in London had one now, it was *de rigueur* — and it didn't exactly help his perennial self-esteem issues, not to mention feelings of racial alienation. That's why he hated him even more, but mostly because Greg the City Guy struck him as entirely humourless. How does one get anything done without humour, he thought? Lenny's mother, Dianequesha, had often accused *him* of being humourless, but it wasn't true. Absurbities absorbed, and darker impulses too, some-times. Dianequesha was deeply religious, and his race's relashionship to Jesus was one of the absurdities he pondered. Imagine if whites had never realised that Africa was resource-rich and entirely lacking Jesus: we we doing fine before. Then you enslave us, eventually "free" us (on your terms) and leave us enslaved in another way, the way of the dependent mind, Christ-sold.

Lenny, we should say, was lovelorn. Ah, so sweet. And yes it was, up to the point when when thought became obsession, or stalking became selective walking. He smiled quietly at the absurd-ity, remembering the previous week. A week he wished to erase from his soul, if that were possible. Lovelorn could be so curiously close to anger.

On Wednesday morning, he had helplessly (and mortifyingly) declared his love for Abra over her voicemail. His armits were still burning with shame.

That night, by the window with the tiny binoculars and the stretching shadows on the wall, he saw Greg enter Abra's building at ten minutes to ten. Greg, his Urban Nemesis, didn't emerge until seven the next morning. By then the shadows were as long as Lenny's imagination, and growing fouler by the second. There was nothing from her that day.

On Thursday evening he sent an apology text via WhatsApp. It clicked green: received. And what a sap am I? Lenny remembered his Shakespeare lessons at school ... 'You do look, my son, in a moved sort/ As if you were dismayed ...' and the pertinent '... of one who loved not wisely, but too well./ Of one not easily jealous, but being wrought ...' He remembered Dianequesha telling him how Shakespeare was the 'devil's work', and to stick to Biblical texts. She read books with titles like *Darwin And The Myth Of Evolution* and *Four Wings To Jesus: How Homosexuality Pollutes Every-thing* and *Why Open Your Legs When You Can Open The Bible? Let Jesus In*. No wonder they laugh at us, mother: no wonder they think we're primitive. They say we have no culture. We've always trusted far too much — been such talented adorers.

On Friday morning he received the following message from Adora:

205

Lenny, my sweet daring neighbour, who helped me move in when I most neded help: thank you. Please don't hate me for this tardy reply. I've been thinking over what to say. What I should or should not say. I was, and am, truly flattered by you asking me out. You are a nice person and I'm sorry if I was curt or if I made you feel bad. I didn't mean it that way. But the fact is, I have a boyfriend now, and he's a good guy. You both are. And he's your friend. Can we all be friends together? With no bad feelings, please. Please? If you like, come over on Saturday and we can smooth it all out over a little vino. Just me and you. Around 8? Hope this finds you well. Abra xxxx

p.s. you are SUCH a sweet guy, don't do this to yourself

Today was Saturday. Lenny rose at a respectable 10.30 a.m. and retrived his phone from the multi-coloured bedroom bin, where he'd tossed it after Abra's message. Not ready for this. Cracked screen; YouTube flickering. Bathroom. A full twenty minutes scrubbing in the mouth. After a damage-check of his psyche, he donned an outfit — red trousers, white shirt, green jacket, dark thoughts circling. Dianequesha had died a few years earlier, and left him nothing in her will but a Bible quote. He silently recited it, as he took the stairs down, three steps to a stride. *But you, O Lord, are a shield about me, my glory, and the lifter of my head.* She had been disappointed in him. Fuck you, he thought. I'm glad you're dead.

* * * *

Nigel, at that moment, drove on to Redcliffe Gardens, up high at the Earl's Court end of it.

'You know,' said Milo, 'this place is shit without me.' He was referring to Britain. 'Life is far more interesting with me in it. They need me. I'm gold standard talent. Is that it?'

Nigel pulled up outside Abra Greco's house. 'That's it, sir.'

They took it in, slowly, bins to roof. The red dust, the alleys containing empty beer cans, crumpled Marlboro packets, discoloured condoms, broken glass, chipped teeth, dead leaves and the souls of men ...

'Nigel, I know I've never asked like anything of such, like, before, but, like, what do you think? Poss? Obvs? For a burglary? How hard would it be, like?'

The century felt very close. It was all happening, much too quickly, and all at once. Nigel considered the proposition.

Neither man noticed the diminutive black man on the opposite side of the street emerge from number 28 and sway off toward *For The Love Of Sheep*, the pub on the corner of the Fulham Road.

A word on Milo's driver, Nigel. Not simply Milo's driver, he also doubled as his unofficial bodyguard. 60 inches tall, he didn't appear imposing but possessed the body of a Soviet Army Water Transporter. You didn't want to get hit by Nigel: fist of granite. Bushed eyebrows, an ill-advised "curtains" haircut from the 90s, a gumminess about the eyes … and implacable fortitude.

'Nigel?'

'Let me think about it, sir.'

'Drive past again. Go round. Then do it again. Lay of the land. Lay on the land. Whatevs. Innit. Obvs. What *they* say.'

'Yes, sir.'

They circled the block until Milo announced: 'I've had enough. Let's go to the pub. There was one back there. On the corner.'

The car pulled again to the right.

Lenny had by now reached the pub and was greedily savouring a cigarette outside it. Tooooosh. Flooosh. The smoke was his first of the day, and it's worth mentioning the effects of the first hangover smoke. Your body is already rotten with memory, so you spark it with a nonchalant air, knowing what will happen. Despite misgivings (and common sense), you spark it. Give it life, while it slowly takes yours. The inhale surges up your arms, tingling excitingly. Three drags and your chest locks in. A rush of genteel abandon — like being lost and alone in a foreign city, like kissing a girl you never thought you would kiss — fills your soul. This is closely followed by a faintly pleasurable nausea. Forming brain-first, it works its way down until, when you finish the damn thing, you stagger slightly and wish you'd never begun. Tooooosh. Senses being attacked from the heart out. Something pulling you close to the ground.

For The Love Of Sheep was one of the few remaining boozehouses thereabouts that still served proper old-school English pubgrub, the porkpies, cheese and onion slices, scratchings and nuts, Scotch eggs ... As he flicked the soggy fag butt into the gutter and turned to enter, it suddenly occurred to him that Scotch eggs must be the worst possible food for vegetarians ... death on the outside, the possibility of life on the inside. With a last floooosh out, and stifling a half-smile, he entered the pub. Ah, the inviting verbal burble. This is exactly what we need.

'A Shelob, please, Danny. Pint, as always.'

Three steps lower than the street, *Sheep* (as it was known locally), was a standard watering hole that happened to feature some perks. One of these was a charming mezzanine bar, mildly famed for its hipster ales and the proliferation of celebrity comedians who drank there. Another was its ceiling, that all agreed looked like it was from the set of the film *Alien*. Oddly twisted wooden panels in geometric yet vaguely recognisable forms ...

As Lenny sipped his pint, Nigel parked the car. Milo shouldered his way out, a physical rearrangement of some colossal effort, due to the burgeoning belly, but also stress.

'Is that called what it says it says it is?'

Nigel, now also on the pavement, nodded. 'Yes, sir, *For The Love Of Sheep*.'

'Jesus,' said Milo, 'didn't I say, like that's *black* stuff ...'

'I think it's a Welsh pub, sir.'

'Let's go. Innit. I mean, let's go in. It. Go in it. *Jesus*.'

Nigel was a very good bodyguard. Being a bodyguard didn't just entail guarding the person. It meant sometimes making them invisible. This was accomplished by combining exaggerated per-sonal gestures — a confident nod of the head, an expansive arm movement — with shielding the boss's face as much as possible. Misdirection. Nigel was exemplary at this, so no one noticed the two men enter, buy a pair of Shelobs and retire to a back booth, except one.

Lenny, a mere one Shelob deep, noticed. But then Milo was, after all, one of his snooker heroes, along with Johnny *Justification* Farrow and Dave *Just Make Me* Woke. Another beer was called for. Lenny gestured to the barman for drinks to be sent to Milo (and companion). He deftly approached them as the drinks were served.

'I'm sorry to bother you gentlemen, but are you Milo Milkins?'

Milo looked up at the elegant black guy asking him something with a mixture of disgust and fogged amusement. 'Yeah, and?'

'I'm sory to bother you, but if you're Milo Milkins, then you are my hero!'

'*Huh*. Funny. Great. I'm everyone's something these days. Innit.'

'Thanks for the beers,' muttered Nigel ...

'No problem at all, guys. Sir — you really ought to be, no, *will be*, a Sir very soon. I just want you to know that the black community like myself are all behind you, absolutely to the hilt. We saw that bit of smearing they tried to do to your character the other day, and I can tell you, I know what journalists are like — they're cockroaches. One just broke my heart. All scum. May I join you?'

Milo was far from happy, but a glance from Nigel cut him down. 'Tell us what you think ... er ...'

'Oh, sorry, Lenny. Lenny Plinth. I just live round the corner.'

'Really?'

Nigel, who rarely spoke, to anyone or about anything, said: 'Have a seat and tell us all about it.'

Milo's brain finally came to the conversation. 'Wait,' he said, 'let me get *you* a drink. We can chat *journalists*.'

The pub TV was showing (silently) films with titles like *Would You Kill A Child?* and *What Are Those Strange Drops Of Blood Doing On Jenniffer's Body?* and *Slasher In The Morning* on loop. In the mezzanine bar, comedians shouted at each other, tossing a joke this way or that, notebooks at the ready. Hey — If I had a pound for every time women told me they weren't attracted to me, I'd be attractive to women. Hey *hey* — When I was younger, I felt like a man trapped inside a woman's body ... then I was born — hey *hey* ... Even though Jesus was a carpenter, he didn't actually sing on any of their albums ... hey hey, jeeee — Your mum is so stupid she posts Missing Dog posts from other countries ...

Back in the back of the backest booth downbackstairs, realisation dawned on Milo. 'I wanna hear more about your journo stuff ...' he said, and Nigel beckoned for more drinks. In the bodyguard world, that was like announcing yourself. *This better be good*, he thought, itching his left eyeball with an elbow ...

'Well,' began Lenny, 'what would you like to know?'

* * * *

An hour or two later, Lenny got upstairs and paused to regain composure or some such nonsense, self-esteem, or what not. Hey ho. He paused to cough into his sleeve and wipe his nose on it. *It's just a jumper. No damage. Instant wash.* He thought a million things. All of them seemed wrong. He seemed wrong to himself, in body, in spirit. Who am I? What am I? A coloured card half-protruded from under Abra's door. She hadn't been out today. Interesting. He picked it up ...

He can Handle, Remove & Destroy Black Magic, Voodoo, Obey, Witchcraft, Demonic Forces, Evil, Bad Luck & all Negativity and Gives Protection
I can give you 100% Spiritual Reeding
About your problem and help you solve it.
Destroy you problems before they destroy you and live a life of Happiness, peace, love and prosperity like millions of people across the world.

Business Problems
Money Problems
Family Argument
Childless Couples
Love Problems
Enemies
Jealousy
Marriage Problems
Sexual Problems
Property
House Problems
Worried About Loved One
female issues,

Well, that about sums up this evening, he thought. He particularly liked the lower-case *f* for female issues: this *f* in some way balanced that dangling comma at the very end ... Absurbities again. The *Enemies* bit was very good too.

Abra opened the door with a *frish* and a delightful, unreluctant, scattered expression. Genuinely contrite, with warmth in the eyes and sad creases on the shoulders, there and *there*. What would *you* say?

'Please, come in and I want you to sit! Look, cushions. Okay? It'll be good. I'll be back asap!'

Okay.

'Just wait ONE minute! I have a surprise …'

Sure.

I'm trapped in satire, or perhaps farce, Lenny thought, then suddenly realised that he had no idea what either term properly meant.

He simply did what his generation had been trained or otherwise learned to do. Worship the slavemasters, worship Jesus, ignore or forget your antecedents. He got up, grabbed Abra's laptop and phone, tipped them into his bag, listened for a moment (the tinkling of white girl piss on white porcelain) and pulled her front door closed behind him. Everything silent. Then he bolted down the stairs, four at a stride, and out into the blue. For a moment, he was free.

'You got it?' asked the white man.

Milo's car was there, exhaust idling, and the door was open …

'I got it,' replied the black man.

'Get in,' said the white man.

Lenny did as he was instructed.

At that exact moment, Abra emerged from the bathroom on the second floor of 33 Redcliffe Gardens. Laughing, she continued, 'You know that wasn't meant …'

Then she stopped, thinking that Lenny had hidden and was about to jump out, phone in hand, to film her surprise for YouTube, or MeTube as he called it. But she sensed, no, knew there was no riptide of love. No rollers and combers on this one. There was no one there. She cast her eye over the room, astonishingly alone. *Wait.*

Where was the laptop? And where was the mobile? Initial fury subsided into resolution, and then sadness. I gave up myself, my moral character, for this. I became a human for this? I became

211

more than myself for *this*? Contrary to what you might infer, she was referring to journalism. The story that would make her career had just disappeared. More than that, betrayal stung, deeply. She dispelled the natural age-old racist impulses, and sat down to think. Stop shaking and think, stop hating and think. *Why did I ever trust that ...* And there it was again. Instinct. The racist impulse.

She went to look in the mirror. A girl, no, a woman. Worn face, tired cheeks, clear conscience.

She looked in the mirror more closely. A journalist. *Everything for the story, even your family.* An ex-boyfriend had told her this, before he left. Czeslaw Milosz said, famously, 'if a writer is born into a family, that's the end of that family'. Her profession, with the advent of social media, was now dead: history was no longer history, truth was no longer truth, remembering was no longer remembering.

She went to the fridge to get a glass of wine. A £5 bottle of El Bombero. As she poured it she looked at her hands — more like her mother's every day, skin like Bible-paper. But she had no mother to tell. There would be no more mothers, and no more belief. No more of this, or of that.

After he'd given the laptop and phone to Nigel, and received his pocketful of cash, Lenny shook hands with Milo, watched the car drive off, and walked around London Town for five hours. Perhaps he was dying. He didn't care. And neither did anybody else. His dad might have cared, but Lenny's dad was long gone, as was his mum. Lenny had felt like dying for some time. Dying held promises — but of what?

At least he'd met his hero, and shaken hands with him, and his hero *valued him*, as a black man, as a person, as a human. I have something to live for, he thought, and I'm happy to be alive at the same historical moment as the great *Incredible Maelstrom*, saver of black children. As he walked, his brain crystallized — I am lucky, he reckoned. I survived. More, many more, just like me, did not. *Milo saved me, too.*

In her room, Adora smiled at the distance of things: the explosive boredom of what's to come. Her sculpted eyebrows almost took on an expression. She tried a frown. That didn't work either. Blame the brows. Call home. But there was no home to call. She looked in the mirror again: slaked of motion, her face was wan, needy. She saw things in colour, with a quiet voice and carefully formed opinions, all ten fingers twinkling. She tested her feelings on herself, before others. But I hate myself, she thought. I no longer know me. This is what the city does.

Abra curled into the capital letter C, and then, later, G. In that position, on her big new bed with diamond-pattern duvet, she considered her life. What have I done?

* * * *

And Milo once again could pot those difficult-angle blacks square-ly in the jaws, confidently not touching the sides of the pockets, even the pesky middle ones. Black after black after black. On the Seniors' Tour, he rose from a wisful has-been to true champion status once again. His autobiography — the irony — ended up being ghosted. No longer *auto-*, it was called *Milo: A British Hero*. It had a subtitle too: *The Story Of The Man Behind The Charity*. That would be the charity he, or rather his people, set up for disadvan-taged African children. It was awarded the Royal Stamp, the seal of approval all British charities crave, in 2020. Yesterday, it just passed its £40-million mark. You've probably given money to it at some point yourself, as most supermarkets have a collection box by the checkouts. It's the white one with the crossed cues logo — just the right side of patriotic.

And — *wait* — last Christmas Milo *The Incredible Maelstrom* Milkins became *Sir* Milo in the New Year's Honours List. Black-town was right. Milo *The Maestro* perhaps? Whither the Milo?

And he became the face of the government's new thrust for better flood-proof housing. A nationwide campaign, the thrust was to promote bungahighs. Bunga*highs* as opposed to bunga*lows*, or single-storey buildings on stilts, to you and me. Society needs them, as the waters, and the tears, will keep coming. Living on stilts — the perfect solution (and metaphor) for an already teetering world.

Three cheers …

You're going to need it.

Acknowledgements

Thanks to Adrienne 'Ptole' Walters, Allison Baker, Lindsay Bramley and David Danson for helping in the tough times of Covid-19 (when us musicians suddenly found ourselves careerless). Topsy for believing, Rachel Haywood for immortalising me as the face of Coronavirus in her children's book *Ezzy The Virus*, Helen Capper for her work on preparing this book, and SK: 'Always remember the part about love'. Julia Kogan for encouragement, Mike and Rachel for use of their old flat in Switzerland, Terry Allen for use of his tiny ramshackle cottage in the French countryside outside St Malo, Danny C and the team at *North Nineteen*, my local, for allowing me to bogart their barspace for many a quiet afternoon, Tricia L — keep that pen poised — and MA for his longsuffering guidance and advice. Thanks also to my oldest friends, Lenny and Barny — literally born on the same day, and my old mucker, and fellow writer, Will Wiles. A quick shout-out, as promised, to Pietro M ('The Extraterrestrial'), and thank you to everyone at TSL Books, particularly Anne Samson, and to Steve Poulacheris, for his marvellous artwork for this volume — I can hardly imagine my characters any other way now: you have defined them.

I also remember both my parents, recently dead, and my other missing — Paul Applegate, Miriam Murphy, Robert Williams, Angela and John Paul Shemwell, and those lost during the creation, or gestation, of this book — Seán Burke, Ennio M, Ben Golomstock, Tomáš Kutman. You were all loved, and are loved, at least on the dotted line. But Tomáš, up there in the mountains ... You were always joyfully irreverent, laughing and singing: you deserved better than to die there, alone in the snow and ice and wind and water.

A special thank you to Andy Williams (no relation) for his invaluable art and design assistance. Steve Poulacheris and I would like to thank the immaculate models: John Curtis, Harry Flowerday, Maurice Kitchener, Andreas Mavromatis, Samuel Moss, Estelle Rivere, Jo Fisher Roberts ... and especially the deeply missed, one and only David Granville Briggs — *Things just aren't the same at the lake without you, b'wana.*

And now only one thing remains: to close that door ... I don't want to, I don't want to leave you, dear reader ... *Look! There* ... there are our children playing out in the courtyard. An arm is lifted to catch a ball in flight. It is not caught. It clatters on the bins in the corner, an unwelcome sound, and a tiny explosion of yellow leaves. The other children laugh, but not harshly, or for too long. The ball is flung again. It passes, this time — and its aim is true — through us all: me, my friends, my missing. Through lost loves, regrets you say you won't have, loves you hopefully do have, through your missing, your wants. The ball keeps flying until finally it comes to rest in the gloved hand of a little boy. A little boy whose name means *higher* or *ascending*. He catches the ball. It is a good ball, in the present tense. It means something to me too, that ball. It means something to all of us, or it should, but the little boy doesn't know that. All he has is a ball. It's a good ball. Bounces well. Fits in the hand. Prepare to throw the ball again ... *Frish* ...